The gemstone heated up

inside his clenched fist, and streaks of fiery, red light burst out through the cracks between his fingers.

He tried to drop the stone, shaking his wrist as if trying to cast away a bit of mud.

Every crease in his hand filled with red, glowing lava, and at the center, the stone buried itself deeper in his palm, until the stone had burned right into his hand!

Fire spread through his veins, up his arm, and into his chest. And when Milo fell forward, reaching out to grip the table in front of him, the fabric tablecloth smoked beneath his touch, leaving behind a hand-shaped scorch mark.

His body burned from the inside out.

Praise for Nicholas Milano

"A fresh new voice in Young Adult fiction with timeless appeal."

~Award winning author, Linda Bleser

Lavalieres: Gem Haven

by

Nicholas Milano

Gem Haven, Volume 1

Lavalieres: Gem Haven

COPYRIGHT © 2016 by Nicholas Milano

Cover Art by *Debbie Taylor*

The Wild Rose Press, Inc.
PO Box 708
Adams Basin, NY 14410-0708
Visit us at www.thewildrosepress.com

Publishing History
First Fantasy Rose Edition, 2016
Print ISBN 978-1-5092-0764-0
Digital ISBN 978-1-5092-0765-7

Gem Haven, Volume 1
Published in the United States of America

Dedication

To my husband, Jeremey Milano,
who kept pushing me to follow my dream.

Chapter One

Deep down, everybody wants to be special, but it isn't every day this quality can be quantified.

The air was rich with excitement as students piled into the gymnasium. A large banner, hung over the entrance, announced "Lavaliere Testing Today," and featured several painted jewels.

The gym had been elaborately transformed in preparation of the event. Rows of folding metal chairs sat on protective interlocking mats, transforming the gymnasium into an auditorium. Every other light had been switched off, purposely mocking a dimmed atmosphere that cast otherworldly shadows across bleached walls. This was common practice when the school held any kind of major assembly.

A shiver crawled up Milo's spine. He found himself lost in a crowd of students all piling in. He craned his neck, and stood on his toes to get a better look. His friends likely were already here, he just needed to find them. Peeling away from the crowd, he jumped up on one of the metal chairs and got his first good look around the room.

From his vantage point, he could see the stage set up at the far end. A projector screen hanging from the rafters displayed homages honoring the memory of infamous Lavalieres.

These were people who had been respected, revered. They were the special ones, the few who could manipulate nature itself, unlocking hidden abilities within themselves through the bond of a gemstone. They were Lavalieres.

Dwarfed by the screen, a currently empty wooden podium sat beneath a spotlight, framed by two separate Gem testing tables. A name flashed across the screen...

Jesse Sanchez
Age: 42
Gem: Ruby

Milo scanned the rows, looking for any sign of his friends. Lily's vibrant floral dresses were sure to stand out amongst the crowd, but Mark's height and orange-red hair made him a lighthouse in the ocean of students. Butterflies took flight in Milo's stomach as he debated whether he should keep searching or simply find a seat and hope they'd find him.

"And then she said, 'Why don't you just drive to Europe if you don't like flying?'"

Mark's voice rose above the others. He'd just walked in, surrounded by a small group of laughing students. Milo jumped off the chair and caught up to them, feeling much more calm and confident. Milo couldn't understand how Mark could captivate and entertain a whole new group each day.

"What do you expect though, coming from a blonde?" Mark turned from the group and gave Milo a nod of acknowledgment. A few of the others gave Milo a sideways glance and split off.

"Don't let Lily catch you making those kinds of jokes," Milo warned as they continued to their seats.

The class had been broken down by last name and

given cards indicating the proper place to sit. The school was going to extreme measures to make sure everything went off without a hitch.

"Too late, Mark. You do realize that hair color is not an indication of intelligence, right?" Lily's radiant blond locks partially curled at the bottom to round out her chin, and Milo wondered if she mistook the assembly for a photo shoot. He shrank back, avoiding her death glare.

"Yeah, I know, but come on, it's just a joke. Lighten up. I wasn't even talking about you." Mark searched for backup, but by that point many of his groupies had disassociated themselves. Lily fell silent, staring off into the distance. Milo followed her gaze up to the monitor, recognizing the weathered face of the smiling woman. Even from the photograph, the twinkle in her eyes reflected her passion for life.

Rose Flower
Age: 80
Gem: Malachite

Lily bore a striking resemblance to her late grandmother, Rose. Milo remembered her smile and how she was always full of little quips about nature. She was the beginning, the very first person to form a bond with a gem and become a Lavaliere.

As the story went, she had been tending her garden one day when she dug up a small piece of polished malachite and from that day forth she had kept it around her neck as a lucky charm.

Every weed is just a flower looking for a bit more attention.

The malachite was more than just a pendant. It changed her, focusing natural and supernatural talents, allowing them to blossom, bringing her closer to the earth. There was never a day, weather permitting, that Milo hadn't seen her out tending her garden when he visited Lily. The world was surely going to miss her.

"This belonged to her." Lily lifted the necklace revealing an empty crown where the malachite charm once sat. A shadow passed over them, and Milo's attention shifted toward the rafters, but he didn't see anything out of the ordinary.

"Did anyone else see that?" One of the lights above flickered. Milo tried to shake the feeling he was being watched.

"I hear Grandma Rose is pushing up daisies." Zack's obnoxious voice made Milo want to puke. How long had he been standing behind them?

"What do you want?" Mark didn't provide even the slightest hint of patience.

"There will be no doubt of course," Zack grinned, "that I will have the best power in the school. As you know, both my parents are Lavalieres." He winked.

"Being a Lavaliere isn't about showing off," Lily said, gripping her grandmother's necklace tight within her hand. "It's about helping people."

"How did Rose help anyone? Did she keep their plants watered while they went on vacation?" Zack sneered and sauntered off.

Everyone had their own opinions why a bond could occur. If family history played any role in the bonding process, Milo would be at a loss. Neither of his parents had bonded. If he passed the testing today, he would be the first. Lily's grandmother, Zack's parents, and even Mark's uncle had all bonded.

"Honestly, I don't care if I have powers or not, I'm

just glad I don't have to put up with one of Pavlovian's *science* lectures. I think my brain would explode if I had to sit through another one of his childhood stories." Mark tugged at his shirt collar, imitating one of the science teacher's habits.

Milo wished he could feel as calm as Mark seemed. He'd be lying if he said he didn't hope to bond with a gem and gain unique abilities.

"What's wrong with my stories?" Pavlovian came out of nowhere. Milo and the others jumped.

"Nothing, sir." Mark looked like a deer caught in headlights. Pavlovian tightened his jet black tie and made his way toward another group, herding them further inside the gym.

Benjamin Grant
Age: 36
Gem: Sapphire

"Good morning students!" Vice Principal Haley took her place behind the podium.

Milo found her unusually chipper attitude a bit unsettling. Any other day, she'd be scowling and ready to hand out a detention slip to the first person who stepped out of line. Also out of the ordinary, she managed to capture and maintain their attention.

"It's with great pleasure I get to introduce you all to our Lavaliere liaison, Lester Swift. He will be overseeing today's testing. He's here to help coordinate the event and make sure everything runs smoothly. Please give a warm welcome to Swift." Vice Principal Haley started the applause that soon filled the room.

The liaison dwarfed the vice principal and needed to adjust the podium microphone before addressing the audience.

"Thank you. Students of Holyoak High, I'm sure you're all anxious to begin, so I will try not to take up too much of your time. I would like to remind everyone it's possible only a few of you, if any, will form a bond today."

Milo knew the odds were stacked against him, but the smallest spark of hope kindled into a wildfire as he imagined bond powers. Of course most of his classmates likely felt the same way. Even with the excitement building in the room, a pit began to take root in Milo's stomach. No amount of time spent studying the shapes, sizes, colors, and names of gemstones could prepare him for today's test.

"When your name is called, please use the stairs to the left of the stage. Come up to the table and place your hand over the first gem. As you make your way to the other end, the *aurometer* will graph the likelihood of a Lavaliere bond. I will study the results. When you reach the end, please wait for the results to be tabulated. If there are no potential bonds, the screen will flash red. If the screen flashes green, it means a bond is possible. At that point, the screen will show the stone and bond likelihood combination."

Lily's eyes sparkled as she gazed upon the gem-strewn tables. Soon they would be called up on stage and into the spotlight. Of the three of them, Lily had the lowest number and would be called up first. Mark had the highest, and Milo fell in between.

"Thank you for your patience. I would also like to thank all of the staff who volunteered to help us today. Pavlovian and Vice Principal Haley."

Once again, the vice principal took her spot at the podium, this time wielding a very powerful weapon. In her hands, she held a list of names of every student sitting in the auditorium that day. A low hum had taken over the room coming from the people sitting nervously talking to their neighbors. Within moments, this low hum escalated into students "talking" from one side of the room to the other.

Vice Principal Haley set the list of student names down on the podium and attempted to get everybody's attention by tapping loudly on the microphone. It had no effect at first, but soon conversations ceased, and everyone gave her their attention.

"I would like to begin today off with a small prayer." Vice Principal Haley bowed her head and closed her eyes.

"Dear Lord, please help guide our future through the next generation of Lavalieres. Surround them with your grace and keep them all safe." She spent a few more minutes with her head bowed in silence.

"At this time, we will begin with the Lavaliere testing. We will start by calling up Carly Abernathy. Paul Anderson you will be on standby. Everybody should have a number. Please remember your number and join standby at the proper time.

"I would also like to remind everyone, even if you don't react to one of these stones, you shouldn't give up. There are numerous other types of bonding gemstones that aren't being tested here today." She made it sound as though she was addressing the entire group, but Milo didn't need to be psychic to conclude the comments were directed to her daughter, Jessica.

Carly made her way into the spotlight. With all eyes on her every move, she seemed more than a little hesitant. And for good reason, he thought. He'd be nervous too if he had to go first.

She appeared to be completely lost on stage, unsure whether she should begin the test or wait. Milo almost felt bad for her.

"Should I begin?"

"By all means."

She raised her hand and held it about half a foot above the first stone. Only her softly echoing footsteps broke through the eerie silence as she made her way down the line. Milo leaned in, watching and waiting intently, almost expecting something amazing to happen.

Carly reached the end of the table and looked up at the liaison for direction. The screen behind her turned red. She seemed to have a look of relief on her face, but Milo could see the sadness in her eyes.

The next classmate made his way toward the table, and they called another up to the waiting area. When the first reached the end, much to everyone's surprise, the screen flashed green.

Paul Anderson Jr.

Gem: quartz

Bond Potential: 65%

"Congratulations, Mr. Anderson, the first student today with a potential bond. Please follow Mr. Pavlovian. We will need to verify the bond."

Pavlovian escorted Paul away from the stage. After Paul, things moved a bit quicker. One after another, students made their way onto the stage only to wind up with a red screen.

"Jessica Haley, you're on standby." Vice Principal Haley had a difficult time hiding her own excitement.

Jessica received a small hug of encouragement

from her mother. Milo couldn't imagine how nerve wracking it would have been if either of his parents were in attendance.

She stopped at each stone, glancing back for approval before moving on to the next. As she approached the final gem, she appeared to regain much of her confidence. Jessica waited at the end of the table for the liaison to interpret the *aurometer* readings, and she slammed her fist against the table when the screen went red.

Vice Principal Haley abandoned the podium, running over to comfort her daughter. She waved over Pavlovian, who took over the podium, calling the next student up to the waiting area without missing a beat.

Among the three friends, Lily would be the first of them to be called onstage for testing. With only a handful of students left in front of her, Milo could tell she was getting nervous.

"Good luck," he called out, drawing the attention of many nearby students. Lily turned and flashed him a smile, but he could see she was still apprehensive. Milo snuck out of his position in line and made his way up to her.

"It's not going to happen is it?" Lily seemed convinced she was already out of the running.

"Even if it doesn't, it's not the end of the world."

"Easy for you to say, there isn't a single Lavaliere in your family. There's no expectation you'll form a bond." Lily realized what she had said a little too late. "I'm sorry. I didn't mean it that way."

Milo turned to make his way back to his position in line, unsure of what hurt more, her assumption he wouldn't form a bond or the fact she was right. She probably would have followed him if she hadn't been called on standby.

The girl on stage before Lily spent nearly a minute hovering over each stone, muttering something under her breath. Milo wondered if she was attempting some sort of magic incantation. He had heard numerous rumors of methods and superstitions that were supposed to increase the chances of bonding. He couldn't understand why anyone would want to look so ridiculous on stage. No conclusive evidence supported these rituals. Although he didn't plan on doing anything during the test, Milo had been subject to his parents' superstition. They did everything in their power to keep him from coming in contact with gems.

"Is everything okay, Miss Finnegan? Please move it along." The liaison prodded, as he had for other students who had been taking too long.

"My parents gave me a prayer they said would help my chances of becoming a Lavaliere, and I'm going to use it," she replied angrily and moved on to the next stone, only to start the process again.

"We don't have all day, Miss Finnegan. We still have a lot of students waiting," he interrupted. She huffed, but also picked up the pace. She reached the end of the table where she received the bad news. The *aurometer* hadn't picked up any potential bonds.

"It's your fault! You rushed me." The girl stormed off the stage.

Milo gave Lily a smile of support to show there were no hard feelings. She may have upset him, but she was still his friend and he had no intention of spoiling her moment. Lily took a deep breath and made her way up to the table. Milo kept his fingers crossed. Her hand hovered over the first stone, trembling. She lacked her usual strong confidence.

Milo sat on the edge of his seat, digging his nails into the chair in anticipation, waiting for even the slightest sign she might get a green screen.

The process had taken so long for others, it seemed impossible, but within moments she already had reached the far side of the testing table. He realized he had been holding his breath the entire time. And then the projector flashed green.

Lily Flower
Gem: Hematite
Bond Potential: 82%

Even with the proof on the screen, Milo still couldn't believe Lily was going to be a Lavaliere.

Swift stepped up onto the stage to present her with the gemstone. So many questions raced through Milo's head he wasn't sure which he wanted to ask her first. She shook hands with the liaison, while Milo attempted to get her attention. But before she noticed, Pavlovian pulled her off to the side, and the two disappeared out the door on the far end. She never even looked back.

"Of course, little Miss Princess bonded."

"I bet she thinks she's better than us." The comments came from a group a short distance away.

"If not before, she will now. Where do you think she went?"

"She's off to save the world," Zack mocked.

"Shut up!" Mark leapt at Zack, sending his metal chair clanging across the floor where it settled a short distance away. Milo ran over and helped pull his friend off the ground.

"You have no right to talk about Lily that way."

Mark hissed and struggled against Milo's restraints.

Zack sneered, rolling his eyes. He turned to address Milo directly, his fake smile fading fast.

"Try to keep control of your pet," Zack spit the venomous words.

He wasn't sure if Mark broke out of his grip, or if he purposely let his friend go, but in that moment, Mark leapt forward. Zack swiftly sidestepped, faster than humanly possible, and Mark crashed into a group of vacant chairs.

Milo couldn't sit back and let Zack continue harassing his friends. Zack had crossed a line, and seeing Mark on the floor lit a fire inside him. Never before had he purposely joined a fight.

Milo lunged forward and knocked Zack to the floor, the two of them falling into a line of abandoned chairs. A glass vial shattered underneath them.

"Shit! You idiot." Zack pushed him to the side, scooping up pieces of broken glass.

Once the adrenaline subsided, a stinging pain in Milo's palm drew his attention. Light glinted off a shard of glass embedded in his palm. Only a single thought went through his head—he needed to get it out.

With difficulty, he mustered the strength and determination to remove the shard. He reached over and slid the shard up and out of his skin, drawing a bead of blood that pooled in his palm. He tipped his hand and allowed a drop to fall to the floor before he squeezed it tightly shut. Purple rings filled his vision, and his head went light and dizzy at the sight.

"Enough!" Pavlovian grabbed Mark by the arm and hoisted him up on his feet. "I will not tolerate violence. Mark, go cool off in the hallway and return when you have a level head. Zack, clean this mess up and take a seat, I don't want to hear another peep out of you. And Milo, go wait on standby for testing. You're next."

Pavlovian pushed Milo away from the fight and toward the stage. Even as he made his way up to the testing area, he kept glancing back at Zack. He felt Zack's eyes following him all the way over to the stage stairs.

Milo took a deep breath, his head still spinning. Mark hadn't come back, and there was no sign that Lily would be returning any time soon.

"Get up there Milo. Don't be nervous." Even with the microphone switched off, Pavlovian's voice carried through the gymnasium. It was bad enough the front row was already laughing, but Milo's footsteps fell heavy on the creaky wooden stairs as he made his way onto the stage.

Marveling at the vast array of colors, shapes and sizes of the gemstones laid out on the velvety fabric, he recognized a few from pictures, but those pictures didn't do them justice.

At the edge of the table, he took a deep breath and placed his hand above the first stone. He recognized the golden cube as iron pyrite, or fool's gold.

This was it, the moment of truth. Every fiber in his body desperately wanted to bond with one of these gems.

Another crystal caught his attention—a decent sized piece of quartz.

Like the fool's gold, it was also in the shape of a cube. However, the sharp angle of the sides made it look as though it were about to tip over. Quartz came in different colors. This one was transparent with a subtle hint of pink throughout. The light shining down on the stone refracted and cast a small rainbow on the table.

He smiled when he reached the hematite, the stone Lily had bonded with. The hematite on the table looked like a solid round piece of metal, and the reflection off his hand warped on its gray surface. He wanted to pick it up, imagining it would feel cool to the touch.

Milo tried to keep count in his head of how long he took at each one, not wanting to be one of the students who'd be hurried along for slowing down the process.

The next stone was deep purple in color. He recognized it as a bit of amethyst, and hesitated when a shadow flickered across one of the walls, pulling his attention away from the test.

Milo shielded his eyes and looked out at the crowd. Zack was missing.

"Stop the test, something's wrong," Swift announced from his station.

Milo stumbled backwards from the table.

Another shadow flicked, this time across the stage.

Someone grabbed him and shoved something into his hand, but when he looked back, nobody was there.

A sharp pain coursed through his arm bringing his attention back to the object he'd been given. It was a small stone, one that hadn't been on the table. The stone was small and black with globs of red interspersed throughout.

The gemstone heated up inside his clenched fist, and streaks of fiery, red light burst out through the cracks between his fingers.

He tried to drop the stone, shaking his wrist as if trying to cast away a bit of mud.

Every crease in his hand filled with red, glowing

lava, and at the center, the stone buried itself deeper in his palm, until the stone had burned right into his hand!

Fire spread through his veins, up his arm, and into his chest. And when Milo fell forward, reaching out to grip the table in front of him, the fabric tablecloth smoked beneath his touch, leaving behind a hand-shaped scorch mark.

His body burned from the inside out.

The liaison was right, something was definitely wrong.

Milo tried to take a deep breath, attempting to calm himself. He stumbled backward, and collapsed, choking and gasping. He wished for it to end because his body couldn't take much more.

Why wasn't anyone trying to help him?

Chapter Two

Milo first heard the voices around him as distant gibberish until he felt someone raise his wrist.

"The stone is smooth, nearly black," said a girl he didn't recognize from her voice alone, "with streaks of red. Kind of reminds me of lava."

She lowered his hand until it came to a rest on the makeshift table where he now lay. She turned away, and as his vision returned, he recognized her, but only barely. They'd shared a class together. *Abigail.* He remembered how much she hated being called by her full name.

His head pounded as though he'd slammed it between two concrete bricks. His friends' voices were low and muffled from the ringing in his ears, and sounded as though they were at the opposite end of a long tunnel.

Lily jumped up from the floor and said, "I think I found it."

"Yeah, that's the one," Paul and the others crowded around Lily, reading over her shoulder.

"Heliotrope, also known as a bloodstone due to the red inclusions that resemble blood, is one of the rarest bonding gems."

"Where are we?" Milo's head, heart, and hand all pounded in unison. His throat went dry and scratchy.

The classroom around him was in disarray, with

desks pushed off toward the walls and books strewn over the floor. He had seen just about every classroom in the school, but this was one he didn't recognize. The way it was set up reminded him of a doctor's office…and he was the patient.

"Milo! You're awake." Lily handed the book off to the other girl and ran up to his bedside. "Abby, go get Pavlovian."

Milo pulled himself up to a sitting position. He felt dizzy, like his head was trying to catch up after getting off a carnival ride. He clinched the side of the bed and recoiled when the stone smacked against the surface with a small thud. The gem remained firmly lodged in his hand, and along with it, a dull throbbing pain lingered.

"I bonded." Milo stared at the foreign object.

He was still having difficulty making sense out of what'd happened. It wasn't supposed to occur this way.

"What was it like?" Lily took his hand in hers, a sense of wonder and awe coming from the tone of her voice.

"What do you mean? Didn't you bond already?"

She pulled away, shook her head, and said, "Not yet. We get our gems tomorrow morning. We're all wondering where you got a bloodstone. It wasn't one of the gems being tested."

"Join the club. I have no clue where it came from. Everyone knows about this?" Milo raised his hand. The scabbed skin surrounding the gem was rough and sore. He dug a fingernail underneath to pry the stone free, but it refused to budge.

"They know something happened. You can't discreetly pass out on stage in front of an audience and have it go unnoticed," Lily replied with a smile.

She was right. Something happened on that stage. He hadn't seen anyone, but he swore someone grabbed his arm and shoved the stone in his hand.

"It was Zack."

He remembered the way Zack had been eyeing him after the fight broke up, and the strange substance that coated his hand before the test.

"Zack gave you a bloodstone?" Lily looked as though she were having a difficult time believing him. She was one of his best friends.

"I'm not sure. It was forced in my hand while I was testing."

"Impossible, he was nowhere near the stage when you passed out," Pavlovian said as he entered the room.

"He wasn't in his seat."

"He was complaining about a headache after you tackled him, so I sent him to see the nurse."

Milo wanted to argue, but decided to keep quiet. Zack might have been annoying and rude, but he couldn't let his personal disdain for the guy drive a wild accusation. Still, he couldn't shake the feeling Zack was part of it somehow.

"Milo, your little stunt out there is not going to go without its share of consequences. There's a bonding process in place for a reason."

"Yeah, to get us all on some government list so we can be controlled and monitored." Abby pulled her hair back in a ponytail, revealing a streak of red underneath. When she wasn't talking, she went back to chewing on her lip ring.

"Abigail, we aren't inserting a GPS tracker in you. We just need to get a little information."

"Then why can't we have our gems now? He has his." Abby took a step back and crossed her arms, preparing for a confrontation.

"It's for your safety. Understanding how to use a Lavaliere power takes time, and can be dangerous if not handled properly." He paused and turned back to Milo, "Bloodstone is no longer a sanctioned stone. This could be a problem."

"What do you mean?" Milo asked.

"Some gems are more dangerous than others. If you can't control it, well, we'll cross that bridge when we come to it. How are you feeling?"

"Okay, I guess." Milo shrugged, aside from the dull ache in his hand he couldn't complain. The pain actually began to numb. Pins and needles ebbed out from the center of his palm.

"Milo, be honest with me. Have you ever seen any of those gems before today?"

"I've only read about them."

"But you've never come in contact with them?" Pavlovian grabbed Milo's hand and forced it open to reveal the bloodstone. He visually examined the rock.

"No," said Milo.

"Okay, I've got to get out there. I'll be back later to finish up." His teacher left.

When they were sure he was gone, Lily said, "They're worried because you're *leeching*." She failed to conceal her look of concern.

He was familiar with the term used to describe those who formed blood bonds with gemstones to siphon their power. The dangers associated with this type of bonding were often detrimental. Even though the bond was stronger, the stability with a blood bond that could cause powers to go haywire was less. He wanted to bond as much as the next person, but he would never intentionally take on the risks associated with the lack of control that accompanied blood bonding.

"We've known each other since we were kids. Do you really think I would have done this to myself? I wouldn't. You have to believe me."

"I believe you," she said. "I might be able to help. It says in my pamphlet that most hematite Lavalieres have an affinity for health related powers."

"You got a pamphlet about your gem?"

"We all did," Abby said, and she pulled out one featuring a purple amethyst.

"Do I get one?" Milo asked, although he already assumed the answer. Bloodstone wasn't sanctioned. It wasn't part of the test. Therefore, he couldn't expect anybody to have prepared for what happened to him.

"It's not like they are all that helpful. These booklets are so generic it's painful." Paul threw his on the floor. "Lavaliere abilities are diverse. You can't pigeonhole and stereotype a person strictly based on what gem they bond with."

"It would be nice to know a little about my bond though, even if it is just generic information."

Milo frowned. The abnormal circumstances surrounding his bond set him apart from everyone else in the room, and he kind of liked the attention.

"You didn't just bond with the gem, the gem also bonded with you—like a parasite. We've got to find a way to remove it." Lily's expression was filled with compassion despite the way her words contradicted the proposed malicious action.

"No," Milo snapped at her. He wasn't sure where the sudden rush of emotion came from, but he couldn't allow anyone take the bloodstone away from him. "I mean, it might not be a bad thing, right?"

"If it were alive, I'd say it possibly could be a mutual symbiotic relationship. You know, where both organisms benefit from each other."

"Like when bees spread pollen?" Milo surprised himself, having retained some knowledge from one of Pavlovian's many exaggerated lectures.

"Kind of, except more direct, like a sea anemone providing certain fish protection from predators. Although…this isn't alive. And since the bloodstone isn't receiving any benefit, the relationship is parasitic at best. That's why they're called leeches." The two sat in silence until the door burst open.

"The party can now officially begin!" Mark roared as he came bounding into the room, beaming a grin wide enough to make the *Cheshire Cat* jealous. In an instant, everyone forgot about Milo, turning instead on their new guest. They all crowded around, each trying to get a glimpse of the pamphlet Mark held with pride. Adorning the cover was a dark brown stone with golden yellow streaks that ran from side to side in a pattern Milo knew a picture could never gracefully capture.

"That's tiger's eye!" Lily exclaimed.

"Whoa, Milo, what are you doing here? I can't believe you passed out up there."

Milo held up his hand to show the embedded gem, and with the help of the others, filled Mark in on what happened.

"You're a Lavaliere? That's news to me. They've been telling everyone that you were dehydrated and went home."

Milo didn't find this too surprising. Based on Pavlovian's reaction, it made sense they wouldn't run around announcing his status as a leech.

"Who do you think you are? I get called away from my job to find out you've been messing with evil hoodoo?" The man's booming voice silenced the room. Stunned by the sudden outburst, they focused their attention on the door, and the person who stood just beyond.

"Please calm down, sir. If you would just allow me to explain." Pavlovian opened the door wider, and a much larger man burst through.

Milo's first glimpse gave him the impression this was not someone he wanted to cross. Built like an ox, the man had a burly, red beard dusted with a week's worth of old breadcrumbs. His Neanderthal hunched back didn't stop him from lumbering over everyone in the room.

Paul flinched and backed himself deeper into the room. Milo couldn't see any resemblance between the two of them, but based on the reaction and tension in the air, the two clearly shared a history. As the behemoth made his way across the room, Mark gracefully stepped into his path.

"Outta my way, kid," the man said.

"You know, you could seriously use a breath mint," Mark said, and waved his hand in front of his nose.

"What did you say to me?" The guy grabbed Mark by the arms, and lifted him off the floor with ease.

"I said you have very lovely eyes, sir. Would you like to put me down? Maybe we can talk out our feelings."

While Mark kept the guy distracted, Milo and the others rushed to Paul. The kid was visibly shaking, while keeping his eyes focused on the man. Milo's heart pounded in his chest. In his hand, the stone began to radiate heat, with the blood red spots glowing orange.

"No son of mine is going to bring this hocus pocus witchcraft under our roof." The man tossed Mark out of the way and moved to grab Paul.

Milo threw his arm up to shield them and felt the universe bending to listen. The world slowed around them for a mere moment. The air turned tropical within the bubble barrier that formed the shield between the students and the man.

Milo heard his friends' worried screams but chose to ignore them. Power coursed through his veins. It felt good. He could stop this.

Pushing forward with both hands, he met with resistance similar to attempting to thrust through water. The edge of the bubble kinetically drove forward, grazing the man before bursting.

A deep rumbling bellow bounced off the walls. The man's skin reddened, and the hairs of his beard danced as they burned. A small strange looking tattoo appeared as the hair pulled back.

"Milo, stop!" Lily grabbed his arm and pulled him out of the trance holding him captive.

He lowered his hand and dropped to his knees, feeling the rush of energy drain from him.

"You're all the devil's children!" The man scrambled to pull himself to his feet and backed out of the room.

"Yeah, and don't come back!" Mark yelled at the door while rubbing the spot on his arm where the guy's hand had made contact.

"Are you okay?" Lily knelt down next to Paul.

"So…you all met my father." Paul shook his head and kept his eyes fixed on the floor in front of him. "You heard him. I can't go home."

Milo wasn't prepared for the look of disdain Lily cast in his direction.

"What did you do to him, Milo?" She was still frightened, but it wasn't because of Paul's father. He was the reason she was afraid.

"I'm in control—"

"Didn't look like it. And you," Lily turned to Mark, "What were you thinking confronting him like that? He was on the war path." Lily scolded Mark for his childish behavior.

"I'd consider it brave," Mark huffed.

"I'd consider it foolish," Lily countered.

Milo kept his mouth shut and stared at the stone in his hand. He claimed to be in control, but Lily saw right through him. If she hadn't stopped him, there was no telling what he would have done, how far his power would have pushed, or how much destruction he could have caused.

The stone cooled, its colors dimming back to a dull black.

Chapter Three

The smell of the slightest hint of pungent smoke and singed skin still lingered in the air. He'd done it! He'd activated his powers! His heart skipped a beat, or maybe two, as a rush of emotions washed over him. He finally understood the dumb look associated with cavemen in depictions of the discovery of fire. He'd just created fire, from nothing, out of the palm of his hand.

Could he do it again?

Raising his hand felt as if he were attempting to lift a heavy weight. As his adrenaline subsided, the physical drain began to take its toll. He coughed, choking against the pressure on his chest. If he hadn't known better, he could have convinced himself he'd just finished a mile long race without taking a single break.

The room went strangely silent. Milo looked up and saw everyone staring at him as if he'd just grown an extra limb. He took a step forward and the others flinched, pulling back a bit. He wasn't the only one who knew what he was capable of. They'd all seen it. And they appeared to be assessing whether or not they should fear him.

Milo retreated, pulling himself away from the others. Becoming a Lavaliere was all he'd ever dreamed about, and now it was quickly turning into a dark gift, isolating him from his friends. They didn't know what it was like to feel that kind of power coursing through their veins. Surely they would understand once they formed their own bonds.

In the heat of the moment, Milo hadn't noticed Pavlovian's departure from the room. The only other person he could turn to was Lily. She would know how to handle the situation. She'd been his friend forever and had a history of Lavalieres in her family. He looked to her for confirmation and comfort but she turned away, more concerned with Paul and how he was handling the situation.

Pavlovian popped his head back into the room and locked eyes with Milo's. The hairs on the back of Milo's neck stood on end. He gulped, remembering his teacher's warning about getting into another fight. First, he'd been in a physical fight with Zack, and now he'd assaulted another student's father. Even if it had been accidental and self-defense, he'd still be held accountable.

"Milo, please come with me." Pavlovian called him out. This was it. He would be expelled for sure. He prepared himself for whatever punishment he was about to face.

The others gave him space as he made his way to the other side of the room. Mark was the only one who made eye contact as Milo passed.

In the hallway, Pavlovian stopped and said, "That was pretty quick thinking on your part. To have that much control over your bond so soon is practically impossible." His face beamed with the kind of pride one shows to their child after making the game winning play. Pavlovian clapped a heavy hand down onto

Milo's shoulder, and he waited for the inevitable "but—"

"Am I going to be suspended?" Milo's eyes drifted to the floor, his chin being pulled down by the gravity of his offense. The door shut behind them, cutting him off from the rest of his friends. He dragged his feet as they continued down the hallway.

"Under normal circumstances, probably, but I don't think anybody could claim those were in any way normal circumstances." Milo looked up just in time to catch Pavlovian wink. "Don't worry too much about him. This sort of thing happens a lot when students just start out. I'll call in a couple of favors, and it will be handled swiftly."

"Did I just hear someone use my name as an adverb?" Mr. Swift appeared from around a corner. "It's official. We have a total of five new Lavalieres this year."

"Really? Are you sure about that?" The lines in Pavlovian's forehead tightened, becoming more pronounced as one of his bushy eyebrows raised.

"Yes, I have the results right here." Swift pat his pocket and withdrew a small disc. "Of the one hundred and forty-three students in this year's freshman class, we had five test positive, three marked down as possible candidates, and ten no-shows."

Milo rocked on his heels, pretending not to be listening. But one thing Swift said struck him as odd. Why would anyone miss out on Lavaliere testing day? Then he thought about Paul's father's reaction. Maybe other parents kept their kids out of school today to keep them from being tested. The very idea made his blood boil.

"What about a kid named Zachary Sterling? Where did he fall in the spectrum?" Pavlovian's full attention was on Swift. If he wanted to, now would have been the perfect time for Milo to sneak away. He might have too, if he wasn't interested in hearing what Swift had to say about Zach.

Please say he tested negative and will never have another opportunity. Milo secretly crossed his fingers behind his back hoping karma had successfully found its target.

"He was one of the ten students who did not show up when his name was called." Swift's news caught both of them off guard.

"What?" he and Pavlovian replied in unison. They both knew Zach had shown up today, and he was there in the gym during testing. Why wouldn't he have gone up when he was called?

"You two will have to excuse me a moment," Pavlovian said. "Swift, why don't you begin processing Milo, and I'll catch up in a bit?" Then with no explanation, Pavlovian rushed off down the hall, away from the holding room and the gymnasium.

There was only one other place Milo imagined he would head, toward his office along the other corridor. Milo wanted to follow him, to find out what had him moving in such a hurry, but a steady arm on his shoulder guided him in the opposite direction.

"Please follow me. Mr. Pavlovian set me up with a temporary office where we'll need to process a bit of information. Shouldn't take too long."

Swift's request was more of an insistence, given the tight grip on his shoulder guiding him to a room marked by an out of place door he'd never noticed before. It fell directly on the corner of two intersecting hallways, and while there was nothing remarkable about it, simply being unremarkable was what didn't sit well with Milo.

Swift ushered him into the room and closed the door behind them.

Inside, it had the feel of an interrogation room. There was one table and two chairs, but not much else. Swift indicated Milo should take the seat on the far end of the room, and it gave him little comfort knowing the table and Swift would be blocking him if he needed to make a quick exit. He pulled the wooden chair out from under the desk and the legs scraped against the tiled floor.

What if Abby had been right? What if they wanted to get his name on some list, so people like Paul's father could track him down and hunt him in his sleep?

He realized just how silly that sounded, only after the thought had fully taken its course through his head.

"Congratulations. As you may have already heard, your bond is a bit of a special case—the bloodstone, if I'm not mistaken." He waited for Milo to nod before he continued. "It has been a while since we've seen one. We don't even test for that kind of bond anymore."

"It's not sanctioned," Milo repeated the small amount of information he'd gleaned. He leaned back in the chair, affording Swift the opportunity to fill him in a bit more. From the conservative and reserved look, driven by his tightly pursed lips, Milo sensed Swift's reluctance to open up about the gemstone.

"I'm sorry I do not know off the top of my head what power subset is associated with that specific gemstone." Swift cleared his throat, his reaction betraying him in that moment.

"Fire." Milo replied casually. Swift looked up over his horn-rimmed glasses, his tired eyes opened a path for Milo to chip away at the walls he'd put up.

"Oh? Did Pavlovian tell you that?" Swift asked as he carefully folded up the glasses and set them down onto the table. He closed his eyes and pinched the bridge of his nose.

"No, I saw it firsthand." Milo held up his hand and wiggled his fingers.

Swift flinched, his features tightening as he drew in a small breath. Milo frowned, lowering his hand back below the table.

"Hopefully that situation will be corrected tomorrow. Generally, we wait until training has begun before allowing a Lavaliere to be in contact with their gem. Again, this seems like a special case."

Swift swiveled in his chair and opened a drawer, pulling out a tablet.

For the first time, Milo noticed something odd about the room they were in. There wasn't a single window, nor were there any features that indicated this was a teacher's office. With this realization came a sense of claustrophobia.

"There was something else about you that I'd like to talk about before we begin the paperwork. When I was reading the *aurometer,* a fascinating new occurrence came up, something I've never seen in my years performing the test." Swift twirled a fancy silver pen in his hand, masterfully maneuvering it in a manner that captured and held Milo's attention.

"Your readings boggled me, every stone you tested against showed a potential for bonding. A lot of the time we are lucky to see even a slight reading on any given bond. Before you, Lily was the most remarkable Lavaliere I'd ever seen. She showed such a high percentage of bonding ability. But you…do you have any idea why your potential read high with every gem available?" Swift went still, as though he were holding his breath for Milo to grace him with a most profound statement.

"I don't know," Milo admitted with a shrug.

"No, I suppose not. A fluke, perhaps. If you're willing, I'd like to do a few more tests once we're done here." Swift turned the pen around, the opposite side acting as a stylus, and placed it down on the topmost blank line of the electronic form, ready to make the first stroke.

Milo nodded, pretending to understand what Swift was talking about.

"It is also an interesting coincidence that we have a hematite user," Swift mused.

"Why?" Milo immediately thought about Lily and wondered what he had in mind.

"If she's strong enough, she might be able to heal your leeching." Swift pursed his lips and continued by writing Milo's full name down on the pad.

"Wait!" Pavlovian barged through the door and shut it behind him.

Swift jumped at the sudden intrusion, dropping a tablet down on the table with a clatter. The stylus dropped ungracefully and rolled to the floor. A sound permeated the room, one that could strike pain into even the strongest of hearts—a chink of glass snapping as a line formed along the surface of the tablet. The screen went black.

"Sorry, didn't mean to startle you, but wanted to catch you before you started his processing. I need to ask you for a favor. We need to hold off, at least until tomorrow. Do you think we can get an extension?" Pavlovian kept glancing back and forth between the two of them. It sounded like there was something he was trying not to say in front of Milo.

Swift scooped up the tablet and studied the cracked glass as though he hoped staring at it would cause the lines magically to disappear. He toggled and fiddled with every button he could find before giving up on bringing it back from the dead.

"The expected completion deadline is today. An extension might not be possible." Swift appeared torn, his façade cracking like the glass on the tablet. The informal manner in which the two of them conversed gave Milo the impression they were old friends.

"Tell them the tablet broke and you need a replacement. I just need a day or two, that's all," Pavlovian pleaded. Whatever it was that he wasn't talking about, it must have been important.

Milo felt as if he was walking the rope in the middle of their little game of tug of war. He kept hoping to pick up the reason, a small hint why Pavlovian was behaving so frantically.

"*They* know I have a backup. I might be able to buy you a day, but anything beyond that, and *they're* going to get suspicious," Swift emphasized some unknown entity, the recipient of the processing information.

Suddenly Milo was no longer sure Abby's idea of being tracked was so crazy.

Pavlovian nodded his understanding, but it didn't

do much to soften the worry creases on his brow.

"Milo, will you please excuse us. Let the others know that the testing has concluded. We will pick up again tomorrow."

When Pavlovian opened the door and offered him the opportunity to leave, Milo knew better than to turn it down. So he smiled and quickly removed himself from the seat, making his way back into the hall.

He'd made it only a short distance when he tasted something odd on his tongue. He clicked his tongue, wondering if he'd accidentally swallowed a fly. He turned back toward the office he'd just left, but it had disappeared. Or maybe he'd gotten turned around. Milo checked the next three intersections he came to, but he couldn't find Swift's temporary office. He gave up after completely circling the high school and doubling back on the holding room.

Chapter Four

The next morning, bright morning sunlight illuminated the busy hallway. Students milled about, going through the normal beginning of their daily routines, but Milo noticed something had changed. He had never been one of the most popular guys at the school, but now many others appeared to go out of their way to avoid him. The extent of their avoidance went beyond cliques and popularity. It was much more primal than that.

This was fear.

Milo was haunted by the image of Paul's father from the night before. If he hadn't done anything, Paul would have been hurt. He tried to justify his actions, reason with himself. The bloodstone and his ability had been strictly used in self-defense. He needed to remember that what happened had been necessary...a natural reaction.

The pangs of guilt hadn't been quelled for long, when he'd replayed the look of horror on the guy's face, how the man screamed as his skin burned. But in that moment, what worried Milo the most was how he allowed the bloodstone's power to wash over him and how much he enjoyed the feeling of that power.

The bloodstone's activation had been directly tied to his emotions. Now it remained cool and lifeless in the palm of his hand, but when Milo's temper flared, so too had the stone. He let it get out of control once; he couldn't let it happen again.

Milo took a deep and unsteady breath. Almost as if he had forgotten how to remain calm. Even the most basic actions required extra thought. He didn't want to imagine what he could have done if Lily hadn't been there to calm him down.

Mrs. Worcestershire, an older woman with the face of a bulldog, guarded the farthest classroom at the end of the West Wing. She gave his friends and him a glare, herding her morning class in like sheep away from the wolves.

The message seemed clear—they weren't welcome. There was no need to wonder just how fast news had spread, or what kind of rumors were floating around behind their backs. The thought sickened him. The others should speak up if they had something they wanted to say.

"Where are we supposed to meet this morning?" Mark looked around the emptying hallway, but none of them found anything to indicate they were where they needed to be.

"West Wing, classroom A0," said Lily.

"Hate to break it to you, but the classrooms start at A1."

The late bell rang, and the few stragglers lingering in the hallway begrudgingly made their way into various rooms. Only the new Lavalieres remained.

Milo's hand twitched. The bloodstone. Where was Pavlovian? A bit of hope remained to remove the stigma associated with leeching, and that hope lay with Lily getting her hematite.

"You guys wait here. I'll go check his office," Milo

volunteered.

Pavlovian's office was down the B wing, not too far from where Milo thought they were supposed to meet. Every door leading up to the office had been shut, each one representing a normal classroom in session.

He finally came upon an office door that was more decorated than the others in the wing. It was covered from top to bottom with snippets of comics. The door stood open just a crack, and he was about to knock when he heard arguing coming from within.

"You should have been more careful with the last vial."

Milo tensed, unsure whether or not he should interrupt. He leaned in to get in a better position to listen to the argument. To his surprise, Zack was the other person involved in the argument.

"I already told you, Milo broke it when he knocked me to the floor."

Milo fumed. He had half a mind to burst in there, if only to defend himself. He hadn't started the fight with Zack. It wasn't his fault that the vial had broken.

"You will just have to wait. It takes time to combine the chemicals properly. They won't be ready until noon at the earliest. Now, if you will excuse me, I have to present these gems to the new Lavalieres."

Milo scrambled away from the door, not wanting to get caught eavesdropping. He tucked himself into a small nook used to display art. It had also been known as the Kissing Corner due to its small size. The low lighting outside the display cases made it relatively difficult for hall monitors to notice anyone hiding there.

"Just wait until my father hears about this." Zack stormed out of the office. He paused just outside the door, holding up an empty glass vial, he growled and threw the vial at the wall only a few feet away from where Milo was hiding. It shattered, scattering shards of broken glass all over the floor. Zack lurched away, mumbling curses under his breath until he was out of sight.

"A-choo!"

Milo jumped at the sudden sound. He had been caught. His eyes darted in the direction it came from and only released his stifled breath when Abby and Paul appear from the shadows.

Paul was wearing the same outfit from the day before. His hair stuck out at odd angles and there were heavy bags under his eyes.

Abby stood in stark contrast. Every single part of her look appeared to have been planned out to the very last detail; not a single hair out of place and her cheeks gave off the glow one might associate with only a fairytale character that had been in a deep but beautiful slumber.

"What are you three doing here?" Pavlovian asked.

"I was just coming to find you."

"Um...so were we." Abby released Paul's hand. Milo gave them a sideways glance but didn't say anything.

"I'm sorry to have kept you waiting then." Pavlovian slung a brown satchel over his shoulder. The unknown contents rattled inside as they made their way back toward the A wing where the others were waiting. Mark and Lily abruptly ended the conversation they were having.

"Where are we going?" Milo asked as Pavlovian led the group outside. "I'm fairly certain all of the classrooms are in the other direction."

Abby shivered as a cool breeze picked up in the courtyard. Paul shrugged off his jacket and handed it to her.

"Follow me and I'll show you." Pavlovian led them away from the school, crossing the courtyard and continuing toward a neglected field. An old soccer goal stood at one edge, decayed and rusting, neglected when a newer field had taken its place.

Milo was hesitant to follow his teacher into the jungle. His hand brushed up against the wall of weeds. The others disappeared into the brush in front of him. It was now or never. He pushed aside the weeds and stepped forward.

For a while, the only thing guiding him was the sound of his friends' voices up ahead. He was lost in a sea of never ending weeds. Finally, when he was just starting to worry that he'd never make it through, he came out of an opening and fell forward into the group.

In front of them was a sanctuary. Thick walls of overgrowth surrounded the cleared field on all four sides. He could still hear the breeze, but they were protected from feeling its effects. Pavlovian spun to face them.

"Before we go any further, there's one thing I must make clear. Being a Lavaliere is a part of who you are, it doesn't and should not *change* who you are."

Milo knew he was being called out. His teacher made no attempt to disguise this fact by addressing him specifically. He looked away for a moment, ashamed to make eye contact. *I won't let the bloodstone take control of me,* he promised silently.

Pavlovian unbuttoned the top of his shirt and

pulled out a small chain around his neck. The links in the rings looped intricately.

Milo was stunned. He had seen the same type of necklace only once in the past. The pattern matched that of the necklace Lily kept as a reminder of her grandmother. At the bottom, a small charm held an inconspicuous piece of onyx. The flat rock smoothly reflected the sun on its black surface as it dawned on Milo that his science teacher was also a Lavaliere.

"At my core, I am still a scientist, and as such, I have undertaken the task of understanding the bond between gem and Lavaliere..."

Pavlovian turned away from the group and held the stone up in front of him. The world around them grew quiet. Milo noticed the change immediately and drew in a breath.

The night before when his bloodstone activated, it felt as though the universe had leaned in to listen and obey. This felt no different. There was an external pressure that built up like he was hearing everything from under water.

The onyx activated, and a wooden door materialized in front of them. The carved oak frame stood tall and strange against the backdrop of overgrowth. Diamond shaped markings etched along the edges and across the bottom gave the door an even more magical quality. The only marking on its surface was the designation A-0 carved into its surface. Otherwise, it was fairly plain.

"Cool." Mark touched the frame.

Milo and a few others walked all the way around the door. He noted that there was only a single handle on one side.

"Once on the other side of this door, you will be presented with your gems and will join a Legacy of Lavalieres. Go on. Open it."

Logic told Milo there should be nothing on the other side. He would open it only to see the empty field beyond. However, part of him hoped for something more. Just this once logic could take a backseat. He turned the handle.

With a creak, the door opened, and beyond it lay an impossible room. Through the wooden frame, instead of the field, was a classroom the size of a gymnasium.

Milo couldn't believe what he was seeing. It simply wasn't possible. He stepped inside and tapped the floor with his foot, marveling at the sound of his shoes on the wooden floor.

"Welcome to our training grounds," Pavlovian was the last to enter. He shut the door behind them, cutting them off from the rest of the world.

"Why didn't you tell us you are a Lavaliere?" Lily spoke up first on behalf of the group. In all of Pavlovian's stories of his childhood during class, being a Lavaliere never once came up.

"Nobody asked," he replied with a shrug as though it was all that would have been required for him to start rambling. "And because I live for that look of surprise."

Milo's attention was interrupted by a pulsing in his palm. *Not now*, he thought. He looked down at his hand. Hopefully soon it would be separated and hanging from a necklace, like the Onyx.

"If you would all take your seats, we can begin the necklace presentations." Pavlovian motioned to four regal seats set up at the front of the room. The regal red fabric made them thrones fit for kings and queens.

But today Milo was not a king. He was the odd one out. There was no seat for him among the royalty of his friends, since he was not going to be presented with a necklace. Instead, he remained standing while Pavlovian brought out the satchel and revealed the contents.

Even in the dim light, each of the polished links of chain twinkled like stars. There were two chains of gold and two chains of silver. Pavlovian lifted one of the silver chains and stood in front of Lily.

"I present Lily Alexandria Flower, Daughter of Hematite." He placed the chain around her neck. Her eyes closed, like she was asleep, the stone appeared to shine a bit brighter in those couple of seconds.

Milo was happy for his friend, but he couldn't stop thinking about how he may only be moments away from being a normal Lavaliere like her.

"I present Paul Michael Anderson, Son of Quartz."

"I present Marcus Reginald," Mark winced at the sound of his middle name, "Turner, Son of Tiger's Eye."

"And last but not least, I present Abigail Wei Xi, Daughter of Amethyst."

Milo pulled back into the shadows a bit, watching his friends go through this ceremony. He was one of them, a Lavaliere, yet clearly not on the same level. Son of Bloodstone. It didn't even sound as nice as the others. The words seemed tainted in a way.

"You are now officially linked to the Legacy of Lavalieres. To determine the true nature of your abilities, we will need to have some hands on lessons. Would anyone like to go first?"

They all looked eager to get started, but Paul was

the quickest off his chair. He proudly held up his necklace, the crystal clear quartz dangling from the bottom. Milo saw his opportunity to get comfortable in Paul's seat.

"Very good, quartz is a very common bonding gemstone. These bonds fall under a category of transparency and clarity. A good friend of mine from childhood was a Daughter of Quartz. With a proper *flourish,* she could turn herself completely invisible."

"Let me guess. You haven't seen her in years?" Mark slapped the arm of his chair and chuckled.

"No, but it has been far too long." The joke went straight over Pavlovian's head.

"Now then, a *flourish* is the technique used to activate the power of a gem bond. While the activation comes from within, generally a physical act helps a Lavaliere concentrate on what they are attempting to accomplish. This can be anything from simply holding your gem, to something as complicated as performing an interpretive dance. Whatever works for you."

Paul held up his stone, but Pavlovian stopped him. Milo thought back to the day before. He couldn't remember performing any kind of physical action to activate his powers.

"There are three forms that shape your powers. Active, reactive and passive. You saw the active form of my power earlier. I can create these pocket dimensions using my onyx."

Milo found himself checking out the room again. It looked like the inside of a cave with dark stone walls all around. Lanterns, hung every couple of feet, provided flickering light. Pavlovian created it. Milo couldn't even begin to fathom how. His teacher continued.

"The reactive form is exactly what it sounds like when your bond reacts to a stimulus. And the passive form is always occurring. I bet you didn't even notice."

Milo looked around the group, but the others seemed just as confused. He hadn't noticed any passive ability since becoming a Lavaliere.

"Don't worry. The passive form is the most subtle of the three. Sometimes you'll never know what ability comes with the passive form, but believe me, it's there." Pavlovian got that look in his eye, the one each of them knew all too well. He was about to jump into another one of his stories.

"How do we find out what we can do?" Paul jumped in before Pavlovian could begin rambling.

"We have a few methods. The best way is usually to just dive right in. Instinct is key, and we'll begin by trying out your active form."

Pavlovian explained how he had to concentrate, clear his mind, and relax his body. The whole process felt like a study in self-hypnosis.

Paul closed his eyes and took a few deep, steady breaths. He shook off his nerves and held the quartz up in front of him. Time dragged on. The silence meant to help Paul concentrate only appeared to make him more anxious. His face contorted, cheeks flushing red, and his body began to shake.

At first, Milo thought the shaking was an indication of the ability activating, but it became clear Paul wasn't having any luck. With a huff, Paul shook his head and fell back into his chair.

"It's okay, not everybody can do it on their first attempt. Who would like to go next?"

"I'd like to try," Lily offered. She jumped up off

the chair and walked over to Milo. "My power should fall within the healing class. I think I can heal you."

He blushed, realizing that all eyes were on the two of them. This was the moment he had been waiting for all morning. He held up his hand, the bloodstone glowing slightly orange but otherwise inactive.

"Very good. Lily, take hold of the hematite. We will begin with the active form of your power."

Now that the time had come, he was no longer sure if he wanted to go through with this. He wasn't sure it was wise to be the guinea pig in this experiment.

Lily nodded, grasping the hematite in one hand and his palm in the other. Her grip was warm and relaxing. He found his eyes closing as she held his hand. The room had gone quiet, but he didn't care. He was numb, his entire body tingling with pins and needles.

"Concentrate, dig a little deeper." Pavlovian's instruction wasn't meant for him, so Milo ignored them.

"I…I can't." Lily's voice sounded so distant. "He's resisting."

Milo laughed. He wasn't resisting anything. His body went from numb to painful when the pins began to bite at his nerves. She was hurting him. She was doing it on purpose. His eyes snapped open, the room around him tinted in orange, but his attention remained on the girl who was actively using her power to harm him.

She's my friend, his mind fought. His body refused to listen as it writhed in pain. His chest burned and the bloodstone throbbed. He had to make it stop.

A red-tinted, translucent bubble formed around Milo. The bubble crossed at Lily's wrist, burning the skin. She let go with a scream and jumped away from Milo. His body transitioned back to numb before the pain ceased entirely. And once the pain was gone, and the bubble popped. Lily cried out from the floor. Her hand clasped tightly around her wrist.

The result of his actions slowly dawned on him. He had done this to her. He had hurt her. Although unintentionally, he'd hurt his friend. His shoulders dropped. It felt as if someone placed a boulder on top of them before turning up gravity.

Pavlovian rushed to Lily. "This is my fault. I should have realized the shield is his reactive ability."

Milo could do nothing but stare at the wound he'd caused. A simple apology could never make up for what he'd done. He took an uneasy step toward Lily, but Mark stepped between them.

"Why did you do that?" Mark guarded their friend, and the gravity of the situation dragged Milo down. His only friend who could make a joke out of anything, couldn't even make light of what Milo had done.

"It...it was an accident. I didn't mean to." Milo stumbled backwards, away from his friends.

"Enough!" Lily demanded. Her voice echoed through the room. The hematite's metallic surface drew in the surrounding light. Small beads of blood formed around the ring of burned skin. As they watched, her burn bubbled and popped, turning from dark red to a paler yellow scar. It was healing.

"Are you okay?" Mark asked her as if Milo didn't have a right to worry about his friend.

"I will be," she replied. Even with the wound healed, a scar remained. Her wrist was disfigured by waves of skin rising and falling in peaks and valleys.

Looking at the remaining scar made Milo sick to his stomach. He fought the urge to vomit as much as he resisted the urge to cry.

"That will be all for now," Pavlovian sighed and collected the necklaces.

Lily stifled a whimper as she handed hers over.

The room felt larger and hollower as the others filed out.

"Physical pain is only temporary, especially for a hematite Lavaliere. I'd be worried more about the emotional scars. They can last a lifetime if you aren't careful," Pavlovian warned once they were alone. As if Milo didn't already feel like crap.

"I need you to answer me truthfully. Were you in control of the bloodstone yesterday?"

"Yesterday?" Milo wasn't sure how to respond. If he claimed to have been in control, he would be guilty of lying on top of declaring he'd purposely used the bloodstone against Paul's father. Telling the truth, however, would mean admitting his bond had been in control of him.

"I see." Pavlovian frowned, shaking his head.

He had managed to turn everyone against him. First his classmates and teachers, and now even his friends looked at him like he was a monster. He couldn't blame them. How could they trust him? He couldn't even trust himself.

Chapter Five

Milo isolated himself in the boy's bathroom, and hid in a stall, away from his own reflection. He'd burned his best opportunity along with his best friend. Everywhere he went, pain followed.

He punched the wall, grateful for the painful response that resonated back from his reddened knuckles. Lily would know what to do. She always had the answer.

"Hey Lily, sorry I set your arm on fire...can you help me out?" He scoffed at the absurdity of the statement. No, going to her wasn't an option.

The bathroom door flew open, banging into the wall. The interruption drew him out of his private cell. On the list of people Milo didn't want to see right now, Zack filled the top three spots.

Milo turned his back on the intruder, making his way to the sink. He needed to feel the warmth of water against his skin. He tried to turn the temperature all the way up but the stream remained ice cold through his fingers.

"I hear you had a little accident earlier," Zack said.

Milo kept his eyes fixed on the flowing water, calculating his escape route. A single frosted window behind him, or the entrance blocked by Zack, were his only options. His sanctuary became a trap.

"Have you considered just chopping off that hand

of yours? It'd be easy. Just one quick slice." Zack swung his arm down and made a clicking noise with his tongue.

"What's your problem?" Milo snapped. He'd put up with Zack's taunting for years. A terrible thought crossed his mind. For once, he could actually do something about it. His fist clenched, pressing his fingers into the embedded gem. For a moment, he considered how easy it would be to make it look like an accident.

"My problem? Seems like you're the one in hot water." Zack squared himself off in preparation for a fistfight.

"Be careful Zack, you wouldn't want to wind up getting burned." Milo wasn't sure what came over him, but it felt good to have the upper hand, finally.

"Is that supposed to be a threat? You may be a Lavaliere now, but don't think for a second that you are better than me." Zack smirked.

Milo's blood boiled. He raised his hand and willed the bloodstone to activate. Like each time before, he could feel the power manifesting.

Zack's punch connected with Milo's stomach. A resounding *thud* reverberated throughout the bathroom. Milo doubled over, wheezing from the blow. All remnant of the bloodstone's energy dissipated.

"Threaten me with your powers again and not even Gem Haven will keep you safe. I'll chop off that hand of yours myself." As Zack turned away to abandon Milo, a glimmer reflected off a gold chain poking out from beneath his shirt collar.

"Pitiful," Zack added without so much as a second glance, "your *flourish* was transparent."

Milo groaned, struggling to pull himself to his feet. Using the sink as a brace, he took a moment to catch his breath. That chain around Zack's neck…it couldn't be.

Milo followed in pursuit, stumbling out into the hallway. His hand throbbed, as if the bloodstone understood Zack's threat with perfect clarity.

Where did he go? Milo looked around, but Zack had disappeared. The bloodstone still had a faint glow, pulsing with the beat of his heart. There was another option. He didn't need to have the bloodstone, or his hand, removed. He vowed to learn how to control his bond and activate the bloodstone at will.

"There he is. I told you we'd find him before *he* did." Abby's tone reflected the urgency in her brisk stride as they rounded the corner.

"Too late. Zack just left." Milo strained to make sense of his encounter.

"Zack? You've got bigger problems mate." Mark stood between him and Lily.

A buzz of static resonated from the speakers scattered throughout the halls. On the other end Principal Hailey cleared her throat before making an announcement. *"Milo Sylph, please report to the principal's office."* The click designating the end of the message sounded more like a gunshot. A million thoughts raced through Milo's head, but the one that stood out the most was…*Why?*

"It's my father. He's back." Paul glanced over his shoulder as though he expected the guy to be summoned just by mentioning him.

"What does he want with me?"

"Think about it. He may have attacked us, but he's been telling people you assaulted him," Abby's words were jarringly out of place, like they shouldn't have been meant for him.

"But wait, there's more," Mark put on his gameshow host voice. "Tell him what he's won Paul." The rest of the group gave him a sideways glance, and he threw his arms up, backing up a step.

"You know my father is firmly against Lavalieres bonding with stones. He thinks it's the devil's magic." Paul continued to monitor the area as he spoke, "But that's just the tip of the iceberg. He's part of something bigger, something worse. I've overheard him talking at night before, when he thinks I've gone to bed. Have you heard of the Augers?"

Milo shook his head and said, "No."

"Seriously? What? Have you all been living under a rock?" Abby huffed and began to pace. "Augers despise us. Why do you think I didn't want my name on a list somewhere? Augers want nothing more than to eliminate the very idea of Lavalieres and gem bonding. And you've caught their attention." She pointed at him.

"It won't be long before someone spots us or they start looking. We should get out of here," Mark urged as the PA cracked to life once again. *Milo Sylph, this is your final warning. Please report to the principal's office immediately.*

"We need to find Pavlovian." Milo went against his instincts and ignored his summons.

They all agreed if anyone would know what to do, it would be Pavlovian. They hurried down to the B wing, slowing only as they got closer to his office.

Scraps of paper lined the floor of the hallway. A small breeze carried a couple of them a short distance before dying down again. One of the scraps lay motionless at Milo's feet. He picked up the strip and recognizing the science comic as one he'd previously seen hanging on Pavlovian's door. He showed it to the others. Up ahead, the door was partially open.

"Um, I think this is as good a time as any to start coming up with a new plan." Mark stood at the entrance to Pavlovian's office.

"How is that possible?" Abby skid to a halt beside Mark. Her mouth hung open slightly. Milo prepared himself for the worst, dreading what they might see.

What he saw when he arrived was more surprising than he imagined.

The office was gone. Not in a sense that everything had been removed, but rather it just wasn't there anymore. In its place was a small room, no bigger than a broom closet. A small light swung from the ceiling, blinking as it swayed. It brought life to the shadow of an old abandoned mop, the only other item in this otherwise empty room.

"Oh wow, this makes perfect sense." Everyone turned to Lily.

"It does?" Milo asked.

"Of course. I always thought there was something odd about his office. Haven't you ever noticed it from walking in?"

"Proud to say I've spent most of my time here avoiding his office," Mark said with a grin. Lily ignored the comment.

"He created it, just like he did with the classroom earlier today. I should have noticed his office was too big to be between these two rooms, but I'd never questioned it before." Lily looked as though she had just solved a major riddle.

51

"Fantastic, but we still have no clue where he is now." Paul leaned against the wall and folded his arms across his chest.

"Don't you see? We know exactly where he is. I'd bet anything he went somewhere only we could follow him—the classroom." Lily's eyes sparkled with excitement.

"Assuming he wanted us to follow him." Abby pointed out.

"And here I was hoping we would get to skip class today." Mark sighed, shaking his head.

Milo bent down and picked up one of the comics trapped under his shoe. The single frame contained a drawing of a rollercoaster whose car crested the top of a hill. Strapped in from back to front were a fish, a lizard, a rat, a monkey, and a man. The front most seat remained empty. Underneath the picture was the caption—Maximum Potential?

Milo imagined himself in the front of that coaster, hanging over the edge of a large hill with no choice except to be pulled forward into the unknown. A familiar pit in his stomach filled with the conglomerate of anticipation, excitement, and fear.

"There's the leech!" A voice yelled from down the hall.

Milo looked up from the comic to see Paul's father leading a decent sized group in their direction. He recognized many of them as his classmates' parents.

One of them yelled, "Be careful, he's dangerous!"

"That appears to be a lynch mob. Cool." Mark's response to the oncoming PTA, zombie horde caught Milo off guard. There was nothing cool about this.

"This is worse than I thought, and we're useless

without our gems. We have to get to the classroom." Lily pulled his arm, but he resisted.

"I can protect us." The shield he conjured had protected them from this man before. He could use it again.

"It's too unpredictable. You can't control it, and if you hurt anyone, you'll just confirm what they already believe." Lily's lack of faith in him made him feel like a child who couldn't live up to his parent's expectations.

"You guys go on ahead. He's my father. I have to try to get through to him. You go too, Abby." Paul gave her a stern look as she began to protest.

Milo knew they were right, they had to get to the classroom and find Pavlovian. Sticking around meant putting them all in danger.

Lily grabbed his hand, gave another insistent tug, and pulled, rocking him forward onto the balls of his feet. He stalled a moment, feeling her soft skin against his. He realized her trust in his control over his powers couldn't have completely dissipated. Milo made his decision.

They ran.

Chapter Six

The hallway began to buzz as it filled with unaware students changing classes. Milo rolled to dodge one oblivious classmate and just barely managed to keep his balance. Mark helped keep him steady, but the incident had slowed them down. His reaction time wasn't fast enough. His shoulder connected with the oblivious student, sending him to the floor.

"Hey, watch it!" The obnoxious guy he'd collided with looked up to see who had run into him.

Milo extended his hand out to help him back up, and the guy stared at the bloodstone, his eyes going wide. Milo was about to apologize, but the kid scrambled backwards and tripped over an apology of his own before disappearing into the crowd.

"I've got to go back." Abby slowed as they passed by the kissing corner on their way back to the A wing.

Milo began to feel as though they had made the wrong decision as well. Leaving Paul to face his father alone was like sending a sheep to calm a wolf.

"No, the best thing we can do right now is find Pavlovian and get our gems," Lily insisted.

"I don't even know what my power is yet. At least if I go back, I can make sure Paul is okay."

"They are after Milo. We need to get to the classroom while Paul's holding them off."

"I'm not asking permission. Go get our gems."

Abby turned and disappeared into the crowd.

Others were beginning to take notice that something was off, but none of them dared to confront the group.

"Come on, we don't have much time." Lily guided them back to the A wing. Weaving around students to get to a classroom or to the bathroom was always a minor nuisance, but as they tried to push their way through a crowd, it soon became a major inconvenience.

Students, please return to your classes immediately. Milo, turn yourself in. We just need to ask you a few questions. The vice principal's voice came through the loudspeaker. No matter how sincere or how nicely she asked, he would never turn himself in. If his classmates hadn't been looking at him as though he had three heads before, they certainly were now.

"Pavlovian must have known something was up." Lily concluded as they turned the corner of the A wing.

"So he left us here to fend for ourselves?" Mark asked.

"Maybe he had to." A warning bell rang out. The wall of students thinned to reveal Mrs. Worcestershire guarding the exit.

"Where do you think you're going?" She barked.

"To class, just like they told us," Mark replied with a grin. He may have been telling the truth, but she didn't appear to believe him. Her scowl deepened, and she bared her teeth to reveal sharp canines.

"She's an Auger!" Lily exclaimed.

"Seriously?" Milo was confused about how Lily came to that assumption. He glanced over at Mark, who simply shrugged.

"You brats are all the same. Every year you lot are fawned over like you're some kind of saviors. All of you are really nothing more than ticking time bombs. I see the truth. I tried to warn Vice Principal Haley, but she was too caught up in the idea of her kid being special. Now, even she can't turn a blind eye."

"Mrs. Worcestershire, it's me, Lily. How many times have I spent after school helping you tutor students? I used to babysit your kids. You know I'm not a bad person. We just need you to let us through—"

"Don't try to sway me with your silver tongue! Everyone knows he's dangerous. If you want to prove me wrong show me your hand," she snarled and Milo's heart sank.

The whole school must know by now.

He was already forming a response to her accusations, trying to come up with an explanation for the accident that left Lily scarred. There was nothing he could say. He'd either wind up belittling her injury or proving he was a monster.

Lily didn't even hesitate as she peeled back the coat she'd been using to hide her injured hand. Milo forced himself to look at the damage he'd caused, but there was none. He blinked in disbelief. Her hand was perfectly fine, not a single scar or scratch on it. He looked over at Mark, who half smiled and gave him a small nod. Milo wasn't sure whether he was relieved or furious.

"See? You shouldn't always believe in rumors."

The three of them closed in on the exit.

"Don't come any closer, witch!" The teacher pulled out a talisman and held it up to ward them off.

Its intricate design reminded Milo of a Celtic knot.

The spirals seemed to move on their own, captivating him with an impossible hold. The hallway grew warm around them, but his body froze. He blinked and the world slipped away for a moment. A vast emptiness surrounded him, a void crushing him from all sides. Isolation.

A sinking feeling in the pit of his stomach brought about one question. Where was he? A single all-encompassing word came to mind, *nightmare*.

And then with another blink he was back in the hallway, fighting to remain grounded. Wherever his consciousness had travelled was far worse than the experience when Lily had tried to remove his gem.

"What is that?" Mark asked, indicating the impossible object keeping Milo entranced.

Milo could barely hear him, and he was having trouble remaining on his feet. It took all of his strength to keep from losing his hold on reality.

"A Dilution Knot. If made properly, my grandmother told me it can drain a Lavaliere and steal their bond," Lily explained.

"It's working." Mark placed an arm around Milo's shoulder, keeping him unsteadily on his feet.

Milo tried to summon the strength to activate the bloodstone, but he soon gave up, letting his arm fall weakly to his side.

"No, stop!"

"He's a danger and must be destroyed," Mrs. Worcestershire spat, her face red with rage. Her lips peeled back, saliva dripping from her jowls.

"You don't understand. You're making a mistake." Lily tried to reason with her.

This felt like the end. He stopped resisting, and

then his body went limp in the arms of his friends. At least this way he would no longer hurt anyone.

Milo's control slipped away from him. In an instant, his body burned, flames wrapping him from every side. Was it all in his head? He could no longer tell the difference between real life and fantasy, his mind slipping between the two.

"You lot are the mistakes," the teacher screeched.

He closed his eyes and let the inevitable wash over him. His body released all tension, the floor fell out from beneath him, and in his mind he felt as if he floated above the ruckus. The nothingness surrounding him expanded forever in every direction and yet, at the same time, confined him to this prison.

A new and unfamiliar sensation took control. He had a vague sense he was still in the hallway. The prison shrunk in around him, pulling in and compressing his body. The energy built up until it could no longer be contained, and it released with a powerful bang.

Milo blinked, and the world around him came back into focus. His entire body crawled with pins and needles. The fire shield had dropped, but the hallway around him hadn't been left unscathed. The floor beneath him was singed and looked to be the least of the damage he'd caused.

Lily stood over him. Her hand grasped a chain ending with a hematite. The stone's glow gently faded. In its reflection was a soft red flicker.

Milo's hand began to heat up. He flicked his wrist. A flame sparked forward, and an ember shot out from the bloodstone. It whizzed toward the teacher, who attempted to dodge it, and fell to the floor.

Fire scorched the wall directly behind where she had been standing. She was down on all fours, snarling at him. The Talisman, still clasped in her hand, had broken from the chain around her neck and was smoldering. She tried to put it out, but even from where Milo stood, he could tell the design had been destroyed.

Wrapped up, trying to make sense of the scene before him, he almost hadn't noticed the constant steady beat of the fire alarm. Then came the sprinklers. Each droplet of water seared into his skin, sizzling as though it was dropping on a hot frying pan.

He screamed out in pain.

Smoke climbed higher through the hallway, and Milo ran outside, into the open air. He doubled over, coughed, and sputtered...then turned. His friends were not far behind.

"You have your gem?" Milo managed to ask between breaths. Mark said nothing, also struggling to catch his breath. The only one who seemed perfectly fine was Lily.

"Yeah, Pavlovian gave it back to me when I promised... Never mind. Come on, we can't stop now." Lily was already off at a run, heading toward the soccer field.

Milo felt like he'd just finished running a marathon and had been asked to take another lap. His entire body ached, his muscles were cramped, and all he wanted to do was sit down and take a breather. But the fire would only fuel their anger.

He had to push through the urge to slow down. Soon they would reach the classroom. And...then what? It wasn't as if he could hide there forever. In just one day, he went from being a nobody to being wanted for assault, and now, he could tack on arson to his list. He could throw out any self-defense case now. Who would believe him?

The sound of sirens rose and fell in the distance. Each cycle was distinctly louder than the previous. Surprised they had actually arrived without being followed, Milo slowed as they reached the edge of the thick brush.

The three of them pushed through the thick weeds and found themselves back in the open field. Standing within the weedy walls of the sanctuary, the school seemed a million miles behind them. Even the siren sounds were muffled by the overgrowth.

"How did you know she was an Auger?" Mark asked.

"Her earrings," Lily said casually.

"Her what?" Milo wasn't sure if he heard her correctly.

"She was wearing earrings?" Mark asked, confirming Milo hadn't misheard.

"They were designed in the shape of a diamond struck through with an X. That symbol is representative of being an Auger."

A shiver crept down Milo's spine. His eyes immediately drew back to the door in the center of the field. He sensed something wasn't quite right. The door stood cracked open a bit from the frame.

"Someone's here." Milo said.

"Good guess, Lily. Pavlovian did come here." Mark approached the door and pulled it open wide.

Zack stood just beyond the entrance, but he looked different. His smirk wasn't giving off the usual '*I'm better than you*' vibe. The air of confidence was missing.

"You're not Pavlovian."

"No shit, Sherlock."

"Thank you, Zack." A deep and steady voice rose within the room. Milo couldn't see who spoke, but he knew it wasn't Pavlovian. "Please bring our visitors to me."

A cloaked figure sat in Lily's abandoned chair. His low raspy voice made him sound as though he was just getting over a cold. Milo gulped, his feet moving further into the trap while every bone in his body screamed to run away.

Milo spotted the brown satchel in his lap as Zack stepped off to the side. Milo cautiously made his way toward the other side of the room, and noticed Lily's hand slip into her pocket, where she had hidden the hematite necklace after the previous encounter.

Milo readied himself, hoping the bloodstone would react appropriately if necessary. As he approached, the pit in his stomach grew larger.

"Can you feel that Milo? I too am a bloodstone user." The man smiled from beneath his hooded cloak.

Milo stopped. It was true. Somehow he could sense another bloodstone in the room.

"Who are you and where is Pavlovian?" Lily demanded.

Milo was surprised by the power behind her question. He looked over and saw a small bit of movement near the wall where Mark managed to move into the shadows, making his way toward the intruder.

Zack cast a nervous glance toward the door and said, "Father, we have their gems. We don't need them or Pavlovian."

"Come now Zack, show some manners. I'd like to meet his newest recruits." His response almost sounded mechanical. "I am Igneous, Fuser of the Diadem." His words radiated with power.

"The Diadem is a myth," Lily countered.

"So naïve! Do you believe everything you learn from a man who leaves you to fend off Augers by yourselves?"

Mark was getting closer, but every moment threatened his exposure.

"What's a Diadem?" Milo asked, drawing their attention back to him.

"The Diadem is a collection of jewels, not unlike the three I've found in this bag." He reached into the bag and pulled out the quartz. The transparent gem clouded with a thick red liquid filling it up from the inside. The substance had the consistency of blood and pushed out to every edge of the crystal until it had been entirely converted.

"What did you do?" Lily looked as stunned as Milo felt.

"A special poison. Consider it a warning. I'm looking for the stone that's missing from this bag. One of you is a hematite Lavaliere. Turn it over and I'll let the other two go." He held the bag up. Milo avoided looking over at Lily. Only they knew where the hematite was currently.

Mark reached out from behind…

"Father, behind you!" Zack yelled, finally having noticed what was happening.

Igneous pulled the satchel away from Mark, and Mark fell to the floor empty handed.

Milo rushed forward, attempting to catch Igneous

off guard. The bloodstone vibrated faster with every step he took closer to the man.

Mark was scrambling to get back up off the ground while Lily hung back a bit.

Igneous jumped out of the chair, his hood slid off, and Milo got a good look at him for the first time. Two things stood out. First, the sunken, cracked, gray skin around his eyes gave him an undead look. The second was the golden crown sitting atop his skeletal head. The crown contained a ring of interwoven slots, some of which were filled with various gemstones. In the center, a pale white pearl, began to draw in energy.

Milo only had a moment to react when the gemstone released. He tried to call upon his shield, tried to will it into existence, but nothing happened. He strained to move forward, but some unseen force held his body in place.

"Not so fast. There are two stones missing from this bag, one is the bloodstone lodged in Milo's palm, and the second is the hematite. Where is it?"

"Technically, that means there was only one missing stone, not two," Mark called out. The distraction was enough to weaken the hold the pearl had over Milo. Lily must have noticed him regaining control. She took a step forward.

"It's right here," she said as she pulled the necklace out, "and the only way you'll get it is over my dead body."

It worked. Milo was free now that Igneous was completely focused on the hematite.

"Nope, I tried that already with your grandmother. Turns out you need to be alive. But...he doesn't." Igneous pulled out another stone from the bag, this time it was the tiger's eye. The blood red substance began to convert the gem, and Mark let out a howl of pain. He fell back into the chair, his arms twitching violently.

"No!" Lily dropped her guard to run over to Mark. This was Milo's best opportunity. He had to strike now. The bloodstone needed to work this time. *Please,* he thought.

He was amazed when he looked down at his palm and saw the stone glowing bright.

Milo raised his hand without thinking. His friends were in trouble, and he was the only one who could help them. The bright orange glow manifested into a small pool of molten light. Heat radiated from the ball of flame, but his body resisted the burn.

He aimed it at Igneous and released the projectile. The fire flew toward the satchel and nearly collided just when a blast of air hit Milo, knocking him to the side.

In less than a second, Zack managed to cross the room and step directly in the path of the fire. His shoulder took the brunt of the blow, scorching a small hole in his shirt before Milo willed the flame out of existence. Zack fell to the floor, his body writhing and twitching. His eyes fluttered for a moment and then shut when his body went completely limp.

Igneous spared only a momentary glance toward his fallen son before bringing his attention back to the stone. The poison continued to spread through the tiger's eye, darkening the surface with red swirls. Even Igneous appeared to notice the slowed process, taking much longer than it had with the quartz.

Lily continued to hover over Mark, with her eyes closed, one hand grasping the hematite and the other pressing flat against Mark's chest. Her healing slowed the process.

Milo prepared himself to take another shot, but the bloodstone refused to activate. He shook his hand, hoping to bring back whatever caused his *flourish* to work. His friends were still in danger. If it was purely an emotional response, this should have been enough to do it. Try as he might, he couldn't get the stone to react.

Igneous stepped over his son, heading in Milo's direction. Milo stumbled back, realizing he was trapped.

"You really shouldn't have tried that Milo. We could have worked together."

The pearl on the crown began to vibrate. Milo winced, expecting his body to become trapped by the gem once more. However, the pearl didn't activate. The vibration seemed familiar. Milo looked down at his own stone as it vibrated in his hand, he'd almost become used to it at that point. If the pearl wasn't being activated, that meant...

The door to the classroom opened once more. The silhouette was that of the liaison, Swift. Abby stood just behind him, her face puffy and red. Milo's first concern was what had happened to Paul?

"I had a feeling it was you," Swift addressed Igneous.

Milo began to taste something metallic in the air. The putrid, bitter taste made him want to gag.

Around Swift's neck, a small pearl buzzed and glowed. Igneous stopped advancing and shook his head from side to side.

"Hurry, we don't have much time. I manipulated a few of his senses, but it won't be long before he reorients himself," Swift said.

Igneous turned toward Milo with a confused look, and Milo cautiously waved his hand to check his reactions. Igneous simply stood there blinking, but Milo couldn't leave without the satchel.

He rushed forward and stole the tiger's eye, then Igneous dropped the satchel, swinging his arms wildly in front of him, and Milo dodged and scooped up the satchel with the other two gems still inside.

As they ran, Milo pulled out the amethyst and passed it to Abby. Igneous screamed in frustration, and Milo turned in time to see him activate another one of the gems on the Diadem.

Milo slammed the classroom door shut behind them.

"I've got a car parked just outside the barrier." Swift said as he climbed out through the brush.

Milo was more than ready to get away from this place. After the day he'd had, all he wanted was to go home, rest, and stop running. He was sick of being chased. There was just one problem, when they made it to the other side, there was no car in sight.

"Looks like somebody hijacked your vehicle, mate," Mark joked. He still appeared weak, but throwing around a joke was always a sign of improvement.

From where they were, Milo could see a remaining fire truck near the entrance of the school. He was relieved to see that he hadn't completely burned the place to a crisp.

"It's here. You just need to look carefully." Swift reached for his necklace. Milo got that odd metallic taste in his mouth again. A small patch of grass shimmered a short distance away.

"No way!" Mark exclaimed.

Milo had to blink a couple of times to convince himself that what he saw was real. A sleek blue sports car appeared in front of them like a reverse mirage as they approached.

"You have an invisible car?" Mark ran his hand along the frame.

"Not invisible, doofus." Abby rolled her eyes.

"The pearl allows me to manipulate the senses. Comes in handy."

"Is he...?" Lily started but couldn't seem to complete her question. In the front seat of the car, Paul was propped up against the headrest, his eyes closed.

"We were trying to reason with his father. He started screaming and fell to the floor. We don't know what happened, but he's been like that ever since."

"I know what happened. His bond was poisoned," Milo said. He felt his stomach drop as he pulled the blood red quartz out of the bag. Abby snatched it out of his hands while they explained what Igneous had done.

"Is there any way to fix it?" Abby asked, and Milo instinctively turned to Lily.

Lily shook her head and said, "I'm not sure."

"There they are!" A voice called out from a distance away. Paul's father was storming his way across the courtyard.

"Time to run?" Mark asked.

Milo let out a heavy sigh. Running seemed like all they had been doing lately. This wasn't at all like what he imagined being a Lavaliere would be. All day they'd fled from one place to the next.

Milo sighed. "Time to run," he agreed.

"We'll head to my cabin, and I'll transport you all

to Gem Haven in the morning," Swift said as he drove the car off through the field.

There it was again. The *Gem Haven* that Zack had mentioned earlier.

"Where are we going?" Milo asked.

"We created a safe house called Gem Haven. Well…more like a safe hotel. You'll be shielded from Igneous, and the Augers won't be able to find you there."

"Wait, you aren't taking us home?" Mark looked worried.

"They know who you are. Your homes aren't exactly the safest place to be right now. We'll contact your parents and let them know you're in good hands," Swift replied.

"Who cares about my parents? I didn't bring my DS to school today. Think we could make a quick pit stop?" he asked.

Milo just rolled his eyes. Only Mark could be thinking about video games at a time like this.

By time they reached the cabin, Paul still hadn't woken. They carried him inside and set him down on a guest bed. A nagging feeling in the back of Milo's mind caused him to worry about being followed. When he mentioned his concern, Swift reassured him the car had gone through multiple disguises along the way.

The place wasn't all that big. There were only a single main common space and a few smaller, adjoining rooms. The place had the distinct scent of old wood and ash. Milo didn't like the idea of camping in a place like that for the night, but Lily on the other hand, appeared to love every little detail.

"Milo, if I may have a word with you, alone?"

Swift made his way into one of the side rooms.

Milo couldn't imagine there was anything else that could surprise him today. He'd already been chased and attacked, watched his friends get hurt by a crazy man trying to create something called a Diadem, and escaped in an invisible car. Nah, nothing could phase him at this point.

Chapter Seven

Milo studied the glass vial and the olive tinted substance within. A rubber stopper kept the translucent liquid contained. The entire thing couldn't have been any larger than his little finger.

"Pavlovian has been working on this," Swift said. The two of them sat around a small writing desk in the master bedroom of Swift's cabin. The others stayed behind in the common room at Swift's request. Milo watched a trapped air bubble shift from top to bottom when he flipped the vial.

"It's a compound meant to enhance a Lavaliere's natural abilities as an alternative to leeching. The Lavaliere test indicated your system contained traces of the substance."

"I've seen it before," Milo said, and told Swift about the smashed vial he'd seen during his fight with Zack. "What does it have to do with me?" He handed the vial back to Swift.

"We were only testing on Lavalieres who had already bonded with their gemstone. I feel as if there must be a reason you were targeted to bond with the bloodstone, but I can't figure out why."

The two of them sat in silence. Milo wished he could contribute more to the conversation, but he was beginning to realize there was so little he knew. All he could add were observations and events.

"Wait...how do you know Igneous?" Milo asked.

Swift looked like he had been shaken out of his thoughts. He blinked, a crinkle in his forehead deepened.

"He was part of the Inner Circle up until he disappeared six months ago. As you know, he's attempting to complete the Diadem. Pavlovian thought he would be after you, so he had Lily promise to keep you safe while he went back to Gem Haven..." Swift trailed off.

"But he was after Lily, not me." Milo finished. Swift nodded. "What about the Inner Circle, what's that?"

"There's no need for you to worry about them, I've already said too much. We can talk about it more tomorrow when we catch up with Pavlovian at Gem Haven."

Milo understood this as his cue to leave and made his way back to the common area. Mark had claimed a couch and spread himself out on it, already snoring. He was the only one in the room.

A low light snaked out from a side room next to the fireplace. It was the same room they had set Paul in when they arrived.

Milo made his way over and took a peek inside. Lily and Abby were standing around the bed. He crept into the room and made his way to their side.

"It's not working." Abby held Paul's quartz up to the light, still completely red. "We need to get him to a hospital, we can't keep hoping magic is going to be the answer."

Lily mumbled an apology. The hematite remained lifeless in her grip. Milo had seen her use it multiple times now. Every time she had called upon her power, she had held the stone over her heart.

"Are you even trying?" Milo said and immediately wished he could rewind and take it back. Lily gave him one of the death glares she usually reserved for Mark.

"I'm sorry, not all of us can bypass the time and effort necessary to learn a proper *flourish* to control our powers. You have no right to come in here and act like you're better than me when you can't even control yourself." Lily stood frozen over Paul with a bright aura surrounding her. The hematite began to glow, but she didn't appear to notice.

As her angered rant continued, the aura gradually grew brighter and more focused. The familiar silence filled in and highlighted her voice, making it crystal clear. He didn't dare interrupt.

"...and I don't appreciate the accusation!" The hematite released all the energy it had been storing up, targeting the quartz.

"What's going on in here?" Swift said from the doorway. Milo stood there, still afraid to open in his big mouth.

"Paul?" Abby said. They turned toward the bed. Paul's eyes were half way open, and he was stirring. Lily was silent, and Milo hoped that meant she would forget or at least forgive him in light of the recent developments.

They all hoped Paul's sudden improvement was only the beginning, but it was soon clear it was all they were going to get. At Swift's suggestion, Milo and Lily went to find a bed of their own for the night. Mark continued snoring away on the one couch, Lily took a smaller couch nearby, and Milo took the remaining armchair. He hoped he would be back in a real bed again soon.

****

Milo wasn't sure how much he'd managed to sleep before being shaken awake the next morning. Likely, it wasn't long enough. He was sad to see the sun hadn't even risen. He closed his eyes and leaned into the arm of the chair, only to be met with even more nagging shakes.

"Swift says we need to get going. We have to catch a flight out to Gem Haven." Lily pulled him outside to the cool pre-dawn air. Crickets chirped throughout the wood, composing a symphony that only made Milo want to crawl back into bed.

Mark's extra hour of sleep appeared to serve him well as he rushed to open the car door for them. Milo wished he had his friend's energy, still trying to make sense of what was happening.

"Okay, I think we're ready." Swift closed up the trunk and made his way to the driver's seat.

"Aren't we missing a few?" Milo asked through an enormous yawn.

"Paul isn't fit to travel, and Abby decided to stay here with him."

There wasn't much conversation after that as the car sped down side streets toward the airport. Swift actively avoided taking any major roads, even when Mark insisted it would get them there faster.

"You're on the first flight out. Pavlovian sent these boarding passes." Swift passed out the boarding passes.

"You aren't going with us? What do we do when we arrive?" Lily asked.

"A taxi will be waiting for you when you reach

Springfield. I need to stay here and make sure Abby and Paul are okay." Swift pulled Lily to the side and handed her the quartz. "Can you make sure this safely reaches Pavlovian? I'm hoping he might have insight on how to reverse the poisoning."

****

Getting to the front of the security line was a breeze this early in the morning. Milo was the last to hand his boarding pass over to the guard.

"You have been randomly selected for extra screening. Please hold out your right hand for a swab sample." The guard pulled out a piece of gauze. Milo's heart stopped, and he exchanged a worried glance with Lily and Mark. The bitter taste of metal invaded his mouth and caused his tongue to roll involuntarily.

"Please, sir. I need your right hand." She frowned, her eyes darting to the side looking toward an isolated half empty water bottle.

Milo hesitantly lifted his hand and revealed his palm. He did a double take. The bloodstone wasn't there. The gauze swept across the skin, bumping up as it passed over the invisible bloodstone. He was sure the guard would notice something was off, and for a few tense moments he waited. The guard held the swab up and studied it, as if she were trying to convince herself of a reason to hold him back. The test concluded.

"Thank you. You may proceed." The guard signed his boarding pass, snapped off her rubber gloves in an instant, and made a grab for her water bottle to drown out the invasive sour taste of Swift's ability. Milo was relieved as he headed to the final checkpoint and out to the terminal.

A large old-fashioned board displayed the arrival

and departure times of various flights coming and leaving the airport. Through a series of clicks, the board updated to display current information. Milo was busy searching for their flight number when he heard a loud crash.

"Hey, watch where you're going, kid." A store clerk rushed over and, leaving the shaken boy in a tangled mess on the floor, made sure his store's advertising hadn't been harmed.

"I'm sorry," the kid apologized. He appeared to be around Milo's age, and his face turned beet red as he pulled himself to his feet. The cup he'd been carrying was now crumpled, its contents spilled down the front of his white shirt, threatening to leave behind a muddy stain.

Milo just shook his head and turned back to compare his ticket to the departing flights. He committed the terminal and gate number to memory. There was less than an hour before boarding time.

Stores were spread out sporadically along the terminal, each one themed and geared toward a unique customer base. Milo and the others made their way past a tech store, brightly lit with reflective surfaces, giving it a futuristic look. The restaurants were exactly the opposite. They were dimly lit taverns to attract those who had ample time before their next flight.

Vending machines, strategically placed every couple of feet, were filled with important items a traveler may have forgotten. The aroma of freshly baked pastries drew them toward a small store named New Mountain Café. It was smaller than the bookstore and information center it was sandwiched between. The glass display counter pulled them in, each shelf filled from top to bottom with tantalizing treats.

As Milo made his selections, he heard a familiar voice. The stained shirt and crumpled cup proved it was the same guy from earlier. The kid pleaded with the woman behind the counter whose nametag read "Lynn."

Lynn gave a halfhearted smile. "I'm sorry. You'll have to pay for it if you want another one."

"It was an accident. I don't have much cash on me…" He trailed off with a heavy sigh. The waitress remained steadfast in her refusal.

Milo felt bad for the guy. It had appeared to be an accident. Not to mention nobody had come to his aid.

"I'll take care of it," Milo offered and placed the cash down on the counter. Along with the replacement beverage, he ordered himself a blueberry muffin.

"Flight 1310 is now boarding at gate C8," an announcement said over the loud speaker.

"Shoot, that's my flight. Thank you so much, I hope I can make it up to you someday." The guy grabbed his cup, wrapped his arm around a bag, and ran off through the terminal. Milo was happy enough just to help the guy out.

"Oh crap, that's our flight as well! Didn't the departure board say we had an hour?" Mark asked.

"All flights board at least a half hour before their departure time," Lynn replied.

They thanked her and ran off down the hall, skipping over the other stores along the way.

A flight attendant stood at a podium next to the gate. To their relief, the gate was still open, and a few passengers were still being ushered aboard. Milo and his friends skipped to the back of the line and handed over their tickets to the attendant when they reached the podium. As she passed each barcode under the scanner, the machine made a short confirmation beep, and she followed up with an impersonal, "Have a nice flight."

The passageway to the plane was much cooler than the airport, and Milo was thankful for the warmth of the muffin. All he had to do now was board, get a seat, and eat his breakfast.

Unfortunately, nothing was ever that simple. The noise level of the passengers, many of whom had already nabbed the best seats, matched that of a boisterous crowd.

"Thank you for joining us this morning. As a reminder, this is a full flight so please find a seat and make room for those still boarding."

While trying to head toward the rear of the plane, Milo dodged a couple children running through the aisle. Mark managed to nab an empty seat near the front, and Lily took a middle seat between a larger man and a bouncy little kid.

Milo continued on and spotted an open window seat in one of the final rows at the back of the plane. He made his way toward the row, grateful not to be stuck in the middle seat for the trip, and glad he'd finally be able to enjoy his muffin.

"Excuse me. Sorry. Just need to…oops."

He recognized *stained shirt's* voice. A dull thump hit Milo from behind, sending him tripping into the person in front of him, but it was too late to react. The mouthwatering blueberry muffin soared from his grip, landing upside down on the floor. Even as he reached to salvage the pastry, the person he'd bumped into backed up and squashed it under his foot.

"I'm so sorry," *stained shirt* said.

Milo mourned the loss of his breakfast. "It's okay." His stomach growled in protest.

"Oh, it's you! Thank you again for earlier. I swear I'll make it up to you, and that as well." He pointed to the crumbled mess.

Milo shrugged and continued to make his way to his prized seat. At least he would still be able to ride comfortably, and he always had the salted peanuts to look forward to.

"Looks like we get to sit together. I was asked to move from my first choice to make room for a guy's wife. Oh, my name's John by the way."

Milo made an effort to grunt or give a nod every few breaths. He stepped into the row to claim the seat next to the window.

"Oh, um, I hate to ask this, but would you mind letting me sit there?" John lowered his head.

Milo had reached his breaking point. "Yes, I do mind," he said, surprised he managed to keep himself in check.

"Oh, okay."

Milo thought that would be the end of the conversation, but John managed to ramble on throughout the entire takeoff.

"We have reached cruising altitude and your pilot has decided to turn off the seatbelt sign," the flight attendant announced to everyone's relief.

"Is that a bloodstone? I think we are headed to the same place." John pulled out a piece of quartz from his pocket.

Even with this realization, Milo still wasn't in the mood to make small talk. He nodded and turned away from his neighbor.

His reflection stared back at him from the window. Puffy, white clouds covered the world below. Just as he thought he'd have a moment to enjoy some peace and quiet, John tapped his arm. Milo turned and saw a small cart in the middle of the aisle being tended by the flight attendant.

"Would you care for a snack?" the flight attendant passed him a small bag of peanuts. As she extended her arm, a small bracelet slid out from under her suit's cuff. He caught a glimpse of the charm dangling from its band, a small diamond with lines cutting through. Her eyes lingered on his hand a little too long. She'd seen the bloodstone.

"Auger…"

"Are you sure?" John whispered back, cutting his one-sided conversation short. Milo nodded, trying to hide his hand, but the damage had already been done.

A scream pierced through the pressurized cabin. Both he and John were on their feet without hesitation.

"She's hurting someone." John said, brandishing his quartz like a weapon.

"We don't know for sure." Milo didn't want to cause any more of a scene than they already had, but John appeared ready to jump into the fray. The flight attendant Auger loomed over another passenger only a few rows up.

A small group had already begun to surround the area. Milo couldn't make out the situation from his vantage point. Before Milo could stop him, John pushed his way out of the row and up the aisle.

****

They all crowded around a small wooden security

table. A small fan whirred in the corner. One blade, heavier than the rest, made the whole thing wobble and pump out a beat. Milo kept his eyes on it, avoiding the gaze of the flight attendant standing in the corner glaring at them.

"Okay, explain it to me one more time. What happened?" The security guard picked up his notepad. He'd been scribbling down notes every time they walked him through the events on the flight.

"We heard a scream," John started.

"And you thought Miss Grace here was attempting to assault one of the passengers."

"I didn't," Mark jumped in.

"Right, you've already mentioned that." The guard scowled.

"Just wanted to make sure it was on record." Mark smiled and leaned back in his seat.

"This isn't a trial. Please continue."

"So, I went to help. Being a Lavaliere, one of my responsibilities is to make sure no harm comes to any Inert."

John had used that term a few times already, and every time it drew a scorned grimace from the attendant. He'd explained it as any person who isn't or couldn't be a Lavaliere. Every mention of them being Lavalieres made Milo twitch. They had meant to keep it under wraps while they traveled to Gem Haven, but John was doing his best to make their status known to any and everyone.

"And about when did you become involved?" the guard asked Milo.

"I went to make sure John didn't hurt himself." *Or anyone else*, he wanted to add.

"But you didn't make it over to the passenger?"

"Because I tripped," John said.

"And what was it that you tripped on?"

"I think it was a blueberry muffin."

Milo sank in his chair.

"Okay…" The guard sighed as he wrote it down. "Where do the two of you come into all of this?"

Lily replied, "I've been trained in CPR and recognized the passenger was choking. I rushed over and assisted Miss Grace."

"I watched," said Mark.

"That's not true," John said, shaking his head.

"He didn't watch?" the guard asked.

"No, Lily didn't use CPR to help the passenger. She used her power," John replied.

So much for trying to remain discreet.

"I don't need any help from *your kind*." Miss Grace seethed. Her cheeks flared. The Auger bracelet was now clearly in view.

"Okay, I think I've heard enough. You four can go," the guard dismissed them.

Milo couldn't have been more relieved.

"What? Why?" Miss Grace's eyes widened in disgust.

"It doesn't sound as though they did anything wrong. They were all trying to help, and I believe them."

"You're being fooled, tricked by their magic," she argued.

Milo didn't need to be told twice. He left before she could sway the officer into holding them there any longer.

"Strange," Lily said once they got a decent distance

away from there. "Did anyone else notice he was no longer interested in what actually happened?"

"That's my fault," John said, biting his lip.

"Did you use your quartz?" Mark asked and John nodded.

"People have an easy time believing what I say, and it's easy to influence them. My powers are based in truth and transparency."

"I didn't feel a *flourish* though. When did you activate the quartz?" Lily asked.

"It activates whenever I correct someone else's lie. That's why I needed to tell the guard you used your powers on the guy in the plane." John shuffled alongside as they followed the marked signs leading them out of the airport.

"My hair is blue!" Mark shouted, drawing the attention of those hanging around the lobby.

It took a moment for Milo to understand what he was doing.

"No, it's brown," John said.

"Bawk! Hey, did you just make me squawk?" Mark put his arms behind his back, pretending to be a chicken.

"No…" John replied.

"Come on, you could have at least played along."

"Actually…I can't. It's the drawback to my power. I can't tell a lie anymore," John admitted.

Milo thought he detected a hint of sadness.

"There, I see it. The marked taxi over there should take us directly to Gem Haven." Lily pointed to a green and red-checkered cab. It looked like it had driven straight out of a Christmas commercial. Milo was more than a little anxious to get some answers finally.

Chapter Eight

The same thick clouds Milo had seen from above now blanketed the sky, blocking out the sun. He was convinced they found the correct cab when they approached and saw the name, Swift Services, stenciled on the doors,

"So wait. You have to answer every question honestly?" Mark couldn't seem to wrap his head around the revelation.

"Yes. Every Lavaliere has a drawback, like a weakness. Honesty is my drawback," John said through clenched teeth.

"What's your middle name?" Mark asked.

John hesitated before answering, "Tanner."

"Can you do anything else?" Mark pressed.

"I can tell when someone thinks they are telling the truth."

"A human lie detector? Cool. That could be handy."

The hipster leaning on the side of the large cab tapped his watch. His greasy slicked back hair curled around the arms of his horn-rimmed glasses.

"Well, look who finally decided to show up. Come on, we're wasting gas. Got a long trip ahead of us."

"How did you know it was us?" Milo asked, wondering if the driver had some sort of power.

"Come on. Group of kids, at an airport, without

any luggage, on a school day? Couldn't have made my job any easier." He winked.

"Shotgun!" Mark yelled and made his way to the front, only to be stopped by the driver.

"Not so fast," he said, blocking Mark's path. "Ladies first. Name's Riley by the way." He opened the door and helped Lily inside, his gaze never drifting off her.

"Gladly. Looks like it's going to be cramped back there." Lily grinned and pushed past Mark, who groaned as he accepted his backseat fate.

The tires squealed when the cab peeled out into the main thoroughfare, dodging pedestrians and luggage as they went. Milo gave a small tug at the seatbelt to verify it was secure, as he counted multiple run stop signs. He couldn't help but wonder if taking his chances with the Augers might have been safer.

Milo pressed himself up against the window. Looming skyscrapers compressed the cab from every side. The trip went a bit smoother once they passed the city limits, and each back road began to blur together. The only noticeable change was the distance between each building they passed.

Pattering rain fell from the dark gray clouds overhead, and the constant swish of windshield wipers created a soothing lull. Milo fought the urge to close his eyes, certain that staying awake was the only thing keeping them from getting into a terrible accident. Mark's snoring broke up the monotony, giving Milo a shot at remaining alert.

Lily and their driver were deep in conversation, but Milo couldn't hear it well enough to join in. Even John's seemingly infinite energy had drained, and he too crashed mere minutes into their excursion.

How is it they actually managed to get comfortable enough to fall asleep? The thought trickled through him like the rain running down the window. As if sensing Milo was thinking about him, John stirred and shifted, coming to a rest on Milo's shoulder.

Milo shrugged off the intrusion, pressing closer to the door. He leaned his cheek up against the window and jumped in shock to the ice-cold glass. The jolt startled John out of his slumber, rocking him back into Mark.

"Hey! Watch it, Handsy." Mark shoved John off him.

"I'm sorry, it was an accident."

"Yeah, we've heard you say that a lot today." Mark rolled his eyes and glared out the window.

"It's the truth."

"I know," Mark huffed, the bags under his eyes zombified his reflection.

Milo ignored the confrontation. They'd be over it soon enough. He placed the back of his hand on the window and recoiled, a cold burn mark left behind slowly faded.

"Strange…"

John placed his hand on Milo's forehead. "Milo, you're burning up. Do you feel okay?"

Milo swatted John's hand away and said, "I feel fine."

"I believe you," John confirmed.

"Maybe it's your drawback," Mark said, still pretending to show little interest in the conversation.

"What do you mean?" Milo asked.

"You're a pyro. Think about it. The Human Torch,

Inferno, every fire type Pokémon ever. They all have weakness to cold and water. That's geek 101 right there. You can bet if I knew what my powers were, I'd already have a complete list of my weaknesses and know how to overcome them."

"You don't know what your power is?" Riley asked. "You know, we've got a game we like to play at Gem Haven that helps people learn their abilities. Would you be interested?"

"What kind of game?" Mark asked.

"It's a training game, team based, called Gembreakers. There's a tournament this weekend, but today is open practice. If you want, we could form a team after we get you guys checked in."

"We should really prioritize finding Pavlovian as soon as we get there," Lily said.

"That's not going to be possible," Riley announced as he banked into another tight turn.

"What do you mean?" Lily asked.

"He left for the day and said he had some urgent errands to run or something. I don't think he'll be coming back today." Riley's eyes lingered on the rear view mirror longer than Milo was comfortable with. The car began to swerve toward the sidewalk.

"We'll do it," Milo jumped in and was relieved when Riley turned his attention back to the road.

"Sure, why not? Sorry Lily, I can't keep waiting. I have to find out what my powers are," Mark said.

"Fine. If you're certain he won't be back today," Lily said as they pulled up onto a side street, skidding to a stop in the middle of nowhere.

"We've arrived," the driver said, although Milo noted the closest building must have been a half mile or more down the road.

Giant pines lined the woods, but no path appeared to cut through into the forest like it had at Swift's cabin. Milo shivered as the cool air cut to his core. For the first time, he felt legitimately afraid to step out into the pouring rain, remembering how the sprinkler had felt.

He was just getting the courage to exit the vehicle when the driver walked up to his side carrying a yellow umbrella. "I think you'll need this more than the rest of us."

Milo thanked him and grabbed the handle, grateful for the protection. John fell back, walking alongside Milo as the group followed the driver toward the cover of the woods. Milo held the umbrella out as far as he could without exposing himself.

"So, do you like my friend Mark over there?" Milo watched John squirm.

"When he isn't cranky, I think he could be a good friend, but he's not really my type..." John's voice cracked. Milo thought he caught John giving a wayward glance toward Lily. Milo smiled and gave John a small nudge.

"Oh? What *is* your type?" Milo asked. John slowed a bit, kicking a pebble across the pavement. It came to a rest just behind Lily's heel.

"You are," John whispered and clamped his hand over his mouth, eyes widening.

Milo stopped at the unexpected response, unsure how to respond.

"I'm sorry. I swear I wasn't trying to make this awkward." John attempted to back-peddle, but the statement was already out there and couldn't be taken back.

"No, I'm sorry. I didn't mean to force you to out yourself." Milo worried he'd taken the joke a step too far.

"Thanks, your honesty is what I like most. You aren't fake like others have been. Maybe we can keep this just between us though? I get the feeling Mark would have a field day if he found out..." John put on a weak smile, which only served to make Milo feel worse. Had they made that bad a first impression?

"Sure." He gave John an awkward hug and the two of them continued on, letting the conversation drop. Even through the silence, he felt a shift in the air between them. John held his head a bit higher, and Milo noticed his bright blue eyes were no longer filled with sadness.

The road ended abruptly. The heavy metal aftertaste in the air cued Milo to the idea there was more here than he could see. A doormat adorned with the words "Beware of Dog," lay on the sidewalk where pavement met grass. But there was no door. Milo concentrated on pushing through the illusion, forcing his eyes to reveal the hidden.

There it was, one of Pavlovian's doors. "Welcome to Gem Haven."

Milo took in the wonder of the place as he shook off and closed the umbrella. Large chandeliers that hung from the ceiling reflected in the smooth gold-flecked black, tiled floor. Thick, ivy wallpaper crawled up otherwise plain beige walls. Fancy faux oil paintings hung between baroque lanterns. On the far side, a wooden counter completed the look and feel of a hotel lobby.

"Combining Pavlovian's ability to create pocket

dimensions with Swift's ability to trick the senses. Together, they created the safest sanctuary for Lavalieres."

They approached the counter and the woman seated behind it looked up from her computer monitor, her fingers hesitating over an abandoned keystroke. Milo caught a glimpse of the Sudoku puzzle poking out from under the keyboard. She slid some papers on top of it to cover it up.

"Hey, Nina, are you busy?" Riley asked.

"Not really. What's up?"

"It's getting worse out there. There have been three separate attacks this week alone."

She clicked her tongue and pulled out a small pile of clipboards from a drawer behind the counter.

"I'll need your names, ages, and gems. Oh and don't worry about the room information. I'll add it once you've been assigned."

Milo took a clipboard and filled in the required portions before handing it back.

She swiped the key cards through the reader and frowned when the computer beeped in defiance.

"It looks like we're running short on single rooms at the moment. I can put two of you in the same room. I hope that won't be a problem."

"Shotgun!" Mark nabbed the key to the single room, leaving Milo and John to each accept a key to the double.

As Riley explained how they could get to their rooms, he caught sight of a girl in a skintight, red tracksuit descending upon the group.

"I see you've picked up another band of misfits. Already traded in your last set of losers?" she asked

Riley. It took Milo a moment to realize she was referring to him and his friends.

"Nice to see you too, Sophia," Riley said. Nina rolled her eyes and turned back to the computer, suddenly very interested in not being part of this conversation.

"I've got the courtyard booked all day for Gembreaker practice. I plan on winning the upcoming tournament. Feel free to come see how much stronger Team Jackal is without you." She strode off, disappearing behind a set of double doors.

"I never liked her," said Nina as soon as she was out of earshot.

"You were on a team with her?" Mark asked incredulously.

"Worse...she's my ex-girlfriend. I may have been the captain of Team Jackal, but she was the one calling all the shots."

"I'd like to knock her cocky butt off of her pedestal," Nina said.

"You may get that chance. Think Gina would like to join us in a practice match?" Riley asked.

"Come on, it's Gina you're talking about. She'd never turn it down." Nina turned back to the computer, her fingers flying across the keyboard. If Milo hadn't known any better, it might have looked like she was busy at work. "Gina's good with it."

"Cool. Do you have a spare copy of the rules?" Riley asked.

"They don't know how to play?" Nina fell back into her seat, looking a lot less excited. She slid open a drawer and pulled out a small packet of heavily creased papers. The single staple clasping them together appeared to be near the end of its lifespan. Red ink scribbled out portions on the front page, with handwritten changes along the margins.

"This is the only copy I have currently." She handed it over to Riley.

"It'll do. Probably best if they watch a match first anyway." He rolled it up and stuck it in his back pocket.

"I'll have to meet you at the courtyard after I find someone to cover my shift. Shouldn't take long. See you guys soon."

Riley led them away from the front desk and toward the double doors. As they made their way through the lobby, Milo couldn't shake the feeling there was something off about the place. Then it dawned on him, there wasn't a single window. It had seemed so convincing as a hotel, he'd forgotten they were in one of Pavlovian's rooms.

Riley stopped for a moment, scanned his room key against a pad on the side of the double doors, and elicited a faint click. They proceeded down a hallway and turned a corner, coming up to a door with a little red sign hanging above it that read *Exit*.

Milo heard the chanting even before they stepped out into the courtyard. The group that gathered outside was one of the largest gatherings of Lavalieres he'd ever seen. At least, he assumed they were all Lavalieres.

His attention, however, was immediately drawn to the sectioned off portion. It was easily as large as a basketball court, but instead of a hoop on each side there were groupings of oversized, pillared statues.

"Wow, that storm cleared up fast." Mark shielded his eyes as he looked up.

"Heh, don't be fooled, it isn't real. We're still inside Gem Haven," Riley said. "Try not to think about it too hard, you'll only wind up giving yourself a headache."

"Glad you could join us. I'll show you how a real captain leads." Sophia called out from the edge of the court.

"Captains, take your positions." A voice called out and Sophia turned to shake hands with a girl wearing a blue tracksuit.

They each went to opposite ends and climbed onto the two tallest pillars. The central pedestal rose above the others by a good ten feet. Three smaller pillars formed a triangle around this central one, and Riley explained they were called the defense posts. Each of those gave off a bright white glow.

"The object is to rack up fifteen points. If you want to win, the quickest way is for your attackers to knock the opposing captain off their platform and then activate it to claim it for your team."

"Sounds easy enough. What's the catch?" Mark asked, as the teams prepared for their match. Three from each claimed the defense platforms guarding the central pillar.

Sophia belted out a few commands from her pedestal as two of the players below her switched positions.

"They're the catch. They will do anything to keep the attackers from reaching the captain. They aren't allowed off their defense pillar unless it's been compromised. Claiming a pillar is worth three points."

"I think I'm already lost," Lily admitted.

"Don't worry too much. We're just going to play

for fun and practice. I'll be making the calls, and Nina and Gina will help. All you really need to know is that attackers attack and defenders defend, simple enough. There are many ways to score points, and I don't expect you to memorize them before your first match. Just listen to my instructions, and we'll have a shot. Sophia might be loud, but she doesn't really get the concept of being a team leader."

A whistle blew cutting Riley off, and the noise level grew with cheers. A player on the red team darted straight toward one of the side defenders even before the whistle finished.

"Burke has crossed the center line! There's no turning back now!" An announcer's voice echoed through the speakers behind them.

The defender of the threatened pillar spun on her heels, kicking up dust as a blast of air swirled out toward the attacker, pushing him away. The attacker pulled himself back on his feet and made another attempt to strike the pillar.

"Did she really think they would fall for the blitz? He's being used as a distraction." Riley directed their attention to the other two attackers who were now quietly sneaking up to the center pillar from the opposite side. One of them reached out and tagged the pillar, and as soon as they did, the pillar dimmed.

"Defender pillar claimed! Two points awarded to the red team!" Simultaneously with the announcement, the defender on top of the claimed pillar jumped, knocking one of the team blue members to the ground.

"She doesn't want them to score the bonus point for knocking her off," Riley explained.

Milo thought he heard something snap, and he

looked down in horror at the team red attacker laying lifeless on the ground.

"Kenny has been fragged! One point awarded to the blue team!"

"Oh my God! She just killed him!" Lily's outrage was only countered by the oddly enthusiastic reaction from those watching. Milo felt the world dropped out from under him, but the match continued as though nothing happened.

"What? No. He's fine." Riley furled his brow.

"How the hell can you condone that? What kind of sick game is this?" Lily's breaths shortened, catching in her throat as she choked back tears.

"Wait, he's telling the truth," John said, to everyone's surprise.

Milo refused to take his eyes off the dead body below. As he watched, it began to melt and fade into the floor. The body completely disappeared, leaving no trace behind that it was ever there.

"We're entered for the next match." Nina rounded the corner at exactly the wrong moment.

All Milo could wonder was what had he just signed himself up for.

Chapter Nine

"She killed him." Lily fell to the floor, leaning against the wall of the hallway connecting the courtyard to the lobby. Riley insisted on removing them from the courtyard before they could make a scene. Milo felt like he was going to be sick. He'd seen and been in fights recently, but he could have never prepared himself for what he'd witnessed.

"Calm down." Nina's sweet words floated through the air, echoing off the hallway walls. A slight ringing remained in Milo's ears, but his muscles relaxed.

"He's fine. Do you really think we would continue to play a game that actually kills people? There'd be none of us left." Riley extended a hand to help Lily up.

"Then where is he right now?" she demanded, swatting him away.

"The regeneration chamber. You trained under Pavlovian. Didn't he explain how his dimensions work?"

She shook her head. Pavlovian hadn't told them much of anything before he left. Wiping away a tear, she looked up at John, whose nod of confirmation was more comforting than Riley's insistence and Nina's calming voice. It was affirmation enough for Milo to agree to hear them out.

"I assumed you knew, or I would have given you the full tour before bringing you here. Pavlovian put the same protection on this hotel that he puts on all his rooms. We can't die here." Riley insisted on helping Lily to her feet, but once more she refused.

"What's it feel like?" Mark spoke up for the first time. He'd been strangely quiet throughout, not making his jokes that usually helped ease the situation.

"Hmm? Kind of like falling asleep, and then you wake up. I never really thought about it."

"And you guys are okay with killing each other?" Milo was having trouble wrapping his head around it.

"Not at first. Back when I first arrived, training wasn't a game. It was too formal, people were stiff, and fell into a rhythm they couldn't break. Gembreakers provided a real sense of thrill and consequence. We developed and adapted through competition. It's all about instinct. Our heads get in the way far too often, and in the heat of the moment, you can surprise yourself."

The ringing in his ears disappeared, and Milo caught a flash of green as Nina pocketed her gem. Lily appeared to be in deep contemplation and audibly gasped when the murdered Laveliere came bounding around the corner. The guy bore no sign of the fate he'd met earlier.

"Cool," Mark summed up their sentiments succinctly.

"I don't know." Lily still seemed uncertain, but swayable.

Riley led them all back out into the courtyard to watch the end of the game. Sophia's team confidently walked off the field to another victory.

"I noticed your new team got a bit scared seeing our performance," she teased.

"We…may have to drop out of the next match," Riley announced.

"Oh ho! Don't tell me you guys have cold feet?" She laughed, choking back a snort. Everyone turned to Lily, the only one holding them back.

"Don't think for a second we won't take you down." Lily said, and Mark cheered.

****

"Gems at the ready," Riley announced and they took their places on the court.

Milo's stomach flipped as he made his way to their side of the field. He scanned the faces of those watching, sensing his inexperience, and expecting his demise.

A whistle blew, and at the same moment, a lightning bolt flew above their heads. He ducked, hair standing on end, as another one crackled toward him.

"Guard left!" Riley yelled.

Out of nowhere, a bolt knocked Milo to the floor. His bloodstone buzzed, soaking in the electricity. A guy ran by, paying no attention to Milo, as he made his way toward Nina's pillar.

"Guard left!" Riley yelled again.

John and Lily followed the order, giving chase to their electric opponent.

Milo's first instinct said to follow the orders, but then he saw a shadow glide across toward Mark's pillar. Milo pulled himself off the floor and sprinted, ignoring Riley's commands. He focused through the bloodstone, adrenaline pumping as heat flowed through him.

He raised his hand…and froze in place. Ice spread over him. The frost bit into his skin. With the stone, clenched in his fist, growing weaker, his mind screamed in agony.

"Not so hot now, are ya?" The girl in red whispered.

Milo tensed, mentally preparing himself for the inevitable.

Stop. A voice echoed in his head. At first, he thought it might have been Nina, but there wasn't any ringing in his ears. He obeyed. *Concentrate, together.*

As the ice frosted over his eyes, he stopped struggling and focused. Warmth spread through his body, cracking through the glacial exoskeleton. He burst through, shattering the ice and sending shards flying off in every direction.

Good. He shook off the remaining particles, and the water evaporated into steam around him.

"Milo, three o'clock!" Mark yelled from his post.

As Milo turned, he saw another jet of ice lash out toward his friend's pillar.

Mark gave a mighty roar, leaping as the ice slammed into the post. The ice spread and the pillar dimmed. But Milo was entranced by his friend, who landed with ease on the ground below...on all fours.

Mark's teeth bared, expanding out from his peeled back lips. Stripes of black and orange fur covered his elongating face.

"Help!" John screamed, and Milo snapped back to attention.

A guy on the other team appeared to be playing with John, cutting him off from the rest of the group by backing him into a corner. The opponent rubbed his hands together, generated a glowing bit of energy between them, and unleashed it at John. Another bolt of lightning went flying toward him and missed John by mere inches. His hair stood on end, but he remained otherwise unscathed.

Milo dashed out between John and the opponent, waving his gem through the air.

A shimmering red shield appeared. Milo maneuvered the shield, using it to block the crackling electricity, as it sizzled on the surface. The bolt, once absorbed, released a stronger plume of molten lava back in the direction of the opponent.

Milo stumbled backward, falling into John. Their startled opponent stood motionless, eyes wide, as the magma burned a charred hole through him, smoldered within the middle of his chest. He dropped to his knees and melted into the floor.

John whooped, wrapping Milo in a tight squeeze.

"Oof!" Milo already felt sick to his stomach. He knew he hadn't murdered the guy, but in that moment, he still couldn't believe he might be capable of committing an act with such ease.

"Thank you, I thought I was a goner," John said, and Milo suddenly understood why it had been so easy.

His friend had been in danger, and he did it to save him. Nothing more. Right? Now he began to understand what Riley meant about instincts taking over. But why did it feel so natural?

"Oops, sorry." John let him go, and Milo brushed himself off.

"Yeah, no problem," Milo replied, still a bit shaken.

"John, behind you!" Riley yelled.

Milo saw the shadow appear behind his friend, but he couldn't react fast enough. An ice dagger protruded through John's chest.

"No!" Milo screamed and charged, flames dancing on the edge of his fingertips.

John fell back and disappeared in a heap before disappearing into the ground.

Milo snapped. He glided across the field, sliding on a strange mixture of ice, dirt, and lava. In the blink of an eye, He covered the distance to the icegirl, extended his hands, pushing his foe to the floor. Gripping his hands around her neck, he squeezed.

Kill her, the voice in his head urged.

He thought he saw a smile spread across her smug face. He concentrated, building up the energy within. He squeezed.

"You...were manufactured...like me..." she choked out just before her head separated from her body and melted into the ground.

Milo fell forward, adrenalin coursing through his veins. What did she mean? Manufactured?

"Milo, head back in the game," Riley yelled, but Milo no longer felt like this was a game.

This was combat. This was kill or be killed. And he'd lost his... friend. She took him away. He fumed. He took a sharp breath in. One attacker remained.

Milo heard a fierce growl and saw the final opponent squaring off with a menacing tiger.

The attacker raised an arm and the ground shook. Large chunks of dirt hovered at eye level. With the flick of his wrist, the rocks and sediment fanned out like bullets, spraying in every direction. Mark roared, turning away and raising a clawed front paw to his eyes.

A root whipped up from the ground, wrapping itself around Mark, pulling his tiger friend down.

Another root shot up and entwined Lily, pulling her to her knees. Both were frantically grasping at the vines as the attacker skillfully manipulated the earth.

The courtyard began to shake slowly at first, but the tremors became worse with every passing second. Milo stumbled through the quake. But the effect was like trying to run in a nightmare, he worried he wouldn't be able to reach his friends.

He fell, sliding on his knees, the rough earth scraping them raw. The distance between him and his goal stretched. He couldn't cover it fast enough. A root popped out from the broken ground. It was attached to Lily.

He might not have been able to reach them, but there was one thing he knew would spread faster than he could run. He reached down and ignited the root. The flame crawled forward, eating up all the fresh wood in its path.

Milo dug his heel into the ground and kept his center of balance low as he rushed toward the attacker. He leapt, collided with the guy, and knocked him to the floor.

In his head, this guy represented everything Milo truly hated. He was Zack, always taunting and hurting his friends. He was Igneous, dark and menacing. He was Pavlovian, starting him on this path with no direction. Milo's energy focused in a single effort, connecting with the guy in a single thunderous crack. Milo collapsed and looked around. There was no sign of the guy who once opposed them other than a single charred mark on the ground.

Lily helped Milo to his feet as he searched for Mark. She shook her head. Milo's entire body ached, and his spirit felt crushed.

The crowd was loving this. They cheered on the carnage, wanting more out of the brutal battle being waged in this arena pit.

Milo glanced at the score, 3-4. They were losing.

Nina and Gina stood tall on their pillars with Riley behind them grinning and nodding as though he were proud of what Milo had done.

"The game isn't over," Riley said, and together they looked over at the pillars on the other side of the field.

Their defenders were watching, waiting for whatever Milo planned next. The only problem was he didn't have a plan. He'd completely forgotten there was another aspect to this game that hadn't even begun yet. They still needed to cross the center line and claim pillars for their team if they wanted it to end.

Milo heard the chants, but they didn't raise his spirit in the slightest. His heart pounded against his chest and head, and with each swell, the aching only grew worse. He was spent. The ground below looked comforting, but he knew if he went down again, he wouldn't be getting back up.

Sophia stomped out an order, and Milo wondered if her reddened face was due to the color of her uniform or if she was pissed because he'd managed to take out all three of her attackers.

The middle defender jumped off the pillar. It dimmed as she touched the ground.

"Uh-oh," Lily said.

Their team had gained two points, but Milo knew they wouldn't be in the lead for long.

"Can they do that?" Milo called back to Riley.

"They sacrificed the pillar to gain an attacker. Sophia must be worried." Riley didn't seem too enthused by the strategic play.

Milo took comfort in the fact that it was still two on one.

"Be careful. Count your shadows. Chloe can remove hers and use it to attack," Riley warned.

Chloe pressed forward, and Milo saw she wasn't casting a shadow. Out of the corner of his eye, he saw a dark bit of movement. That's when the pieces clicked into place.

"Chloe cheated," he said. Her shadow had been on their side of the field the entire time, even when she was defending. He'd seen it while taking on the other attackers every time it had flit through his vision.

"Riley, they're cheating." Milo approached the central pillar.

Riley seemed confused, and Milo wondered if he'd heard him. Riley made a motion and a whistle blew.

"Time out requested." Riley jumped down from his pillar, landing with a thud in the soft dirt below.

"What do you mean?" he asked, and Milo told him about Chloe's shadow.

Riley listened intently, never taking his eyes off Sophia. Milo couldn't tell if he looked angry or upset, or if he even believed him.

Riley shook his head and made his way to the center of the court, calling Sophia down.

Milo held back, not wanting to be anywhere near those two when things exploded, and they did explode. It only took a moment for the exchange to go from a spat to a heated argument, each one attempting to yell over the other.

"How dare you accuse us after you turned on us?" she screamed.

"That's how you've been winning so many matches. You've always wanted to bend the rules. I didn't think you would stoop this low."

"Quiet!" Icegirl approached from the sidelines. "We have a problem."

Chapter Ten

"It's Mark, something's wrong." All other conversations and accusations ceased when they recognized the worry in her voice. Sophia and Riley led the remaining members of both teams down the hall and through the lobby.

"I don't know what happened. When he came through…"

The hallway on the opposite side was a mirror image of the one leading to the courtyard. There was very little along the corridor to prove that it wasn't the same. The major difference was the duplicate courtyard exit, and the dented door.

John pressed his back against the door. Milo choked up at the sight of his friend. He rushed over and ran his hand over the area where Icegirl's dagger had penetrated. Then, when he was sure John wasn't injured, he finished the hug from earlier.

"It's nice to see you again, too." John said with a smile. Milo couldn't quite explain his emotional response. He knew Pavlovian's pocket dimension would keep John safe, but he hadn't felt this kind of happiness since he was a young boy seeing his father return home from war.

"He's in there," John said. "We tried to calm him, but he overpowered us."

A ferocious roar came from within, and with John

no longer providing resistance, the door smashed in. John pulled Milo out of the way just in time for the figure behind the blow to stumble forward, an orange blur crashing into the opposite wall.

Mark growled, his furred front paws clawing and scratching at the wallpaper. Mark's face blended with feline features, creating the caricature in front of them. He stood on his hind paws, bent over precariously, his body a bizarre mix between human and tiger. Striped fur outlined his golden-yellow eyes, whiskers jut out from a flattened nose, and a set of rounded ears shifted toward the top of his head.

Icegirl raised her stone, and Mark roared, snapping his razor sharp fangs. He pushed off the wall and fell to the floor, landing on his side. His chest rose and fell in short bursts. The fur covering him sent shining silver waves back and forth.

"Stop, he's hurt." Lily rushed forward and placed a hand on his chest. As she caressed him, the walls felt as though they were folding in. John reached out, bracing himself against Milo.

"Whoa, did you feel that?" he asked.

"Yeah, that's normal when Lily's healing power is active. I still haven't quite gotten used to it," Milo replied.

Mark's breathing slowed, becoming more regular. His back leg brightened in coloration, Milo never would have recognized it was off in the first place, but Lily had and she'd fixed it. The features in his face softened, and the fangs retracted.

"Thank…mew." Mark's voice was still far rougher and deeper than it ever had been, but Milo could make out what the half-human, half-tiger had said.

"Why didn't it work?" Lily jumped to her feet and pinned Riley against the wall. "You said every Lavaliere is safe here. You said when they die, they heal."

"That *is* how it works." Riley looked just as confused as the rest of the crowd that had begun to gather around.

"Then why is he still a cat?" she demanded.

"Lily...I chose this." Mark rose a furred hand to his mouth, still having difficulty forming words.

"You...what?" She stammered, releasing Riley.

"I liked feeling powerful, so I tried to hold onto that feeling during the regeneration." Mark averted his eyes away from the crowd.

"See, that explains it. There's nothing wrong with the hotel's regeneration. He chose this." Sophia turned to scold Icegirl for the interruption to the game.

"No." Lily crossed her arms, unconvinced.

"No?" Sophia looked like she was bracing for a fight.

"I assure you, he didn't choose to come back with a broken leg, multiple bruises, and lacerations." Lily's voice silenced the crowd.

"Okay," Riley said. "I've made a decision. Until further notice, Gembreakers is hereby prohibited," he said, eliciting many groans.

"You can't do that. We have the tournament coming up." Sophia huffed.

"Until we figure out what happened here and get to the bottom of this cheating accusation, I can and will. The tournament is officially cancelled." Riley helped usher the onlookers away from the area.

"You chose to look like this?" John asked, helping

pull Mark to his feet.

He managed to keep his balance for a moment before wobbling, needing support. He closed his eyes, and with a sickening *"POP!"* his legs changed to a more humanoid form.

"That's better. Still getting the hang of it." He chuckled and tested his balance. "Yeah, I like the way I look. I might even keep the fangs if I can learn to talk with them."

"When are you going to change back to yourself?" Lily asked.

Mark lowered his head. "This is me. I understand that meow."

"How does it feel?" John asked.

"Hmm…natural." Mark purred.

"You sure it's not just because you aren't wearing any pants?" John managed to bring a smile to the tiger man's face.

"Ha, yeah that might be part of it." Mark's tail wrapped around his waist. He stood a bit taller, which could have been part of the transformation, or his newfound confidence.

"He's a leech!" Sophia yelled, pointing at Milo.

He pressed the bloodstone against his hip. Her tone caught him off guard, and in that moment, he felt like he was standing in the middle of high school all over again. Everyone stared at him, ready to persecute, not wanting to give him a moment to explain.

"So what?" Mark jumped in to his defense, just as he had so many times back in school.

Milo shrank back behind his friend, feeling weak and vulnerable. He'd done nothing wrong, and yet it felt like just being there was the problem.

"To keep everyone safe is a Gem Haven rule. The last time we had a leech on our team, they lost control during one of the missions." Riley looked pained as he agreed with Sophia.

"Pavlovian must have had a reason for bringing him here," Icegirl said, as though they were contemplating whether or not to let him stay.

You were manufactured...

Her words echoed in his head. She had said it just before she fell at his hand. What did it mean?

"He'll be back in the morning. Until then, I have no reason to believe letting him stay the night is a danger to us." Riley's ruling on the subject seemed final.

John tensed up. Sophie huffed and walked off.

"We should talk. Come find me." Icegirl dropped a key card in his hand and followed Sophia.

"Nina, can you show these guys how to use the elevator to get around, and take them to their rooms?" Riley asked, and before she could respond, he was already halfway down the hall.

"Sure," she replied to nobody. "Follow me. The elevators here are a bit tricky."

Milo didn't believe her until he saw the elevator for himself. It wasn't like anything he expected. There were no buttons designating where they wanted to go, nor any indication of whether they were heading up or down.

"We call it an elevator because it takes us where we want to go. I put you on the same floor, so any of your key cards should work."

She took John's key card and held it up to a small port. A green light scanned the card, a bell dinged and the doors opened to reveal a new hallway.

"Did we even move?" John asked, putting his card back into his pocket.

"Yeah, sort of. I've learned not to question these things too much. A lot of this place was built on whatever Pavlovian thought at the time.

"I guess he thought elevators take too long." Mark joked. Nina explained how they could use it to get around the various locations within the hotel before leading them out into the hall.

"You two are over here, and Mark, you're right across from them."

"Finally, I could use a bath."

Mark escaped to the solace of his own room, and Milo wondered if he meant he was going to shower, or if he planned on bathing like a cat.

"Lily, you're just down the hall a bit, not too far away."

Nina led her away, and Milo followed John into their own room.

Milo plopped down on the first bed he came to, grateful to relax, finally. John slipped out of his stained shirt and threw it over the back of a chair at the nightstand between the two beds.

A window overlooked a pristine lake. The sky was clear, and birds were playing tag. Milo watched in comfort, his legs thanking him for the rest. An eagle flew to the top branch of a tree, let out a screech, spread its wings, and took flight. It wasn't until the same scene occurred a second time that Milo took notice.

"It's just a simulation too, right?" John walked up to the window, staring out across a pristine lake.

Both of them watched in mild confusion. Milo

walked over and tried to find a latch. Instead, attached to the wall right next to the window was a remote control.

"Strange, I guess it's like a television."

He pressed the power button and the picture on the screen shut off. Pressing it again brought back the lake. The remote was a simple one, besides the power button there appeared to be a channel selector and a mute button.

Milo pressed the channel up and the scene updated. The view remained the same, but now rain splashed against the pane. A cool breeze seemed to blow through the room. Pressing the mute button, the room went silent.

"That's just creepy," John said, shaking his head. On another channel was a moonlit blue landscape, complete with chirping crickets. He could almost smell the muggy night air.

He'd been so engrossed in the window he hadn't noticed John had left until he heard the shower running. He punched some numbers in randomly and the scenery changed to that of a dusty, crater-ridden landscape. Dark emptiness expanded from the horizon, and off in the distance a large blue orb was partially lit.

Milo stood up to get a better view and hovered midair for a moment before lightly landing back to the floor.

He used the bed as leverage and launched himself up. Misjudging how much force he would get in a single bound, he had to brace himself before banging his head against the ceiling.

This is amazing! He jumped, easily clearing the bed and stuck a landing in the middle of the room.

He plucked the remote control out of the air and punched in a random number. Gravity rushed back into the room, dropping everything to the floor, and dumping Milo onto one of the beds.

"What the hell just happened?" John emerged from the bathroom, wearing only a white towel wrapped around his midsection.

Milo tried to ignore the fact that his roommate was practically naked.

"It's the window. This is the most amazing thing I've ever seen. Watch."

He changed the channel again and the room darkened. A vast cave expanded in front of them, and the sound of dripping water echoed through the room. The air around them cooled and even felt a bit damp, like they were actually sitting in the middle of a cave.

"Do you know how hard it is to take a shower when you're floating?"

Milo apologized, laughing as John walked back into the bathroom to finish changing. As he did, Milo pulled out the secondary key card and flipped it over repeatedly.

"I think I'm going to go see how Mark's doing," John said as he ran the towel through his hair.

"Oh..." He felt like a balloon in his chest just popped.

"Did you want to come along?" John asked.

"No thanks, I was actually just thinking about heading out." The last thing he wanted was to go over and watch John ogling over Mark's newfound physique.

Milo left John knocking at Mark's door, slightly hoping his new friend would change his mind and tag along with him.

He likes Mark more.

Milo quelled the nagging voice. Who John was more interested in shouldn't matter to him. He had more important things to worry about.

Inside the elevator, he held up the key card, and the doors slid open to reveal a new section of the hotel.

He turned a corner and came to a door matching the room number listed on the key. Not wanting to barge in, he knocked and waited. A latch slid, and a deadbolt clicked before the door opened.

"Milo! It's so good to see you again. Come on in. It's been forever."

"It's been less than an hour," he replied, although if the window could manipulate gravity, maybe it could manipulate time as well.

"You don't recognize me? I guess that's fair. I've been here longer than most." She latched the door and offered him a seat on her couch. He shook his head.

"We went to school together right up until a few years back when my dad decided to make Gem Haven to keep me safe."

"Your dad made this?" Milo sat down on her couch, confused.

"Do I really have to spell it out for you? Does the name Chloe Pavlovian ring any bells?"

As soon as she said her name, it clicked. He remembered the meek little girl who always sat in the far back of the bus, getting picked on for whatever book of the week she was reading. He'd rarely ever heard her speak.

"I remember now. Weren't you transferred?"

"Yeah." She nodded. "Would you call this

anything else?"

Milo couldn't get over just how much the young girl had changed. She'd grown up a lot over the past couple of years.

"Pavlovian, your father, sent you here because of the Augers?" Milo asked.

"No. Augers are a more recent threat. He was protecting me from those who sought the Diadem."

"Igneous…" Milo said the name, picturing his sunken deadened eyes and menacing smile.

"So you know about him. That makes things easier."

"Yeah, we only barely got away." Milo told her about the attack, and she hung on his every word. He made sure to tell her everything, hoping she might be able to shed some light on what exactly was going on with the Diadem.

"You said he was trying to get Lily's gem? That doesn't make any sense." Chloe looked like she had just heard an impossible riddle. She scrunched her face up, lost in her thoughts.

"Mind filling me in?" Milo asked after a moment of sitting there in silence.

"Huh? Oh, sorry. It's just…the Diadem…can only fuse using manufactured gems. From Lavalieres like you and me."

"And he wants to take our abilities?" Milo asked. Chloe looked away, and he felt like there was something she wasn't saying.

"That's what we let people believe. It does bind the power to him, but it does more than that. With each gem he captures, the Diadem grows stronger. The metal acts as a conduit, linking the gems together. If it gets completed…" she trailed off, and Milo wasn't sure he wanted to know what would happen.

"So we have to stop him." Milo concluded.

"We can't. That's why we're hidden here—so he can't get to us. He's too powerful."

"We stopped him once. Swift slowed him down," Milo replied.

"Slowed him down, maybe, but I'm sure it didn't last long."

"You said we were *manufactured*. Why?" Milo asked.

"That's something only my father can answer." As she was replying, a horn cut in, its frequency reminded Milo of the warning issued by radio stations on weather advisories. They both turned to the window and across the bottom scrolled a blinking red message.

"*This is a message from the Gem Haven Early Notification System. Gem Haven is under attack. For more information please tune to channel…*"

"Does that happen often?" Milo asked.

"No, never." She rushed to grab the remote and switched it over to a news station.

Chapter Eleven

"The Predictive Disaster Service has issued a warning. Potential threat levels have been upgraded to orange," said the newscaster through the drawn curtains of the window screen.

"What does that mean?" Milo asked.

"Hell if I know," she replied. Milo's hand buzzed. It had been ever since the match. Up and until now, he'd written it off as adrenaline, but the evidence was too overwhelming to ignore.

"We need to go." There was only one possibility. Igneous had found them. "This is all my fault." He explained the gem connection to Jade as they rushed back to Mark's room.

People were just beginning to emerge from their rooms, each with their own impossible questions. Jade managed to answer each one with a relative sense of ease.

"First defense team head to the lobby…"

"Return to your room…"

"I'm sorry, we don't know when…"

"We're on lockdown, no one in or out…"

Whenever Jade had her hands full, Milo began parroting these responses as they made their way through a sea of confusion.

When they arrived, he found Mark's door partially open. He feared they may have already evacuated, and worried about the difficulty of locating anyone specific within this maze of a hotel.

At first, when he pushed through and saw Mark, John, and Lily gathered around a small table on the far end of the room, he sighed in relief. But then he noticed how close John was sitting next to Mark on the tiny sofa, and his chest felt like it had caught on fire.

"Haven't you guys been paying attention to the window?" he asked, grabbing the remote.

"Nah, it's nicer with it off. No unexpected gravitational shifts." Mark winked, lounging with his legs crossed and hands interlocked behind his head.

"What else did you tell them?" Milo glared at John and felt betrayed.

"Wha...hey! You ran off to be with Icegirl? Can't say I saw that one coming," Mark replied, and Milo felt the blood rush to his head.

"What? No...I...she wanted to talk to me." He tried to defend himself. He had no feelings for Jade. He couldn't make out John's expression, but if he had to guess, it looked like one of disappointment.

"We don't have time for this. Sort it out later." Jade grabbed the remote from his hand and turned on the news.

The warning continued, although with one slight difference, the level had increased to red.

"I'm guessing that's not an indication of how hot it will be today, correct?" Mark asked, his ears perked, tail stiffly rising behind him.

"I told you guys he knew something," John said, and Milo wondered if he was being accused again. "I'm sorry, Milo. I didn't want to worry you. Riley was lying earlier. He did think letting you stay here was going to be a problem," John explained.

"It's Igneous. He's found us." Milo filled them in on what Jade had told him about the Diadem.

"How could he? The transfer here is done under strict guidelines to keep the location a secret," said Jade.

"We have to get out of here. He's after our gems." Lily jumped to her feet.

"We can't. Gem Haven is on defensive lockdown," Jade explained.

"Maybe... it was Riley," John said.

"Absolutely not." Jade replied, reaching for her gem.

"Think about it. He's the one who transports everyone here, he knows the location, and he lied earlier."

"Believe me. Riley isn't the type to betray his friends."

"He quit his original team," Mark reminded her.

"He did that for me," she said, and the room went silent. "He quit the team because Sophia threatened to kick me off if he didn't let her call the shots."

Milo's bloodstone shook, warning him Igneous was growing closer. His first instinct screamed at him to run away as fast as he could, get away from the hotel and all of these innocent people.

No, you must stand and fight, protect them, the voice urged. With each word, the bloodstone lit a fiery orange.

"We should go to the lobby. We can protect Gem Haven together," Milo said.

"We have some of our best down there fighting to keep him from getting anywhere near us. We really shouldn't go walking up to him. Besides, they will be fine as long as they remain within the hotel," Jade said.

"I'm not so sure of that," Lily replied. "I've been thinking about what happened with Mark, and I think I figured it out. He was partially poisoned by Igneous."

"It's okay to tell them." John put a hand on Mark's shoulder, giving him a small nod.

Mark took a deep breath, but turned away instead.

"He didn't choose to stay like this," John started.

"Okay, fine. You caught me, okay? I don't have control over my shapeshifting ability."

"Igneous's poison. I knew you wouldn't want to be a tiger. I promise we'll find a way to get you human again," Lily said, her eyes lighting up.

Mark's ears lowered. "Um…not quite. I wasn't lying about how much more comfortable I feel as a tiger. I was kind of hoping to transform fully," Mark said, and Lily appeared more confused than ever.

"Seriously guys, leave the personal drama for when we aren't in danger. So what you're saying is, if he poisons anyone, regeneration won't work." Jade brought them back on track.

"Yeah, we need to warn them," Milo agreed.

"Anything else we need to worry about?" Jade asked.

"Just a few major problems," Lily said with frustration. "One, he already has the Diadem started, so we don't know what powers he already has. Two, I think he's working with Augers and has been providing them with runes that will take away a Lavaliere's powers. And three, I think they already found us." Lily pointed to the window.

Milo realized it had been a few minutes since he'd

last heard the warning buzzer and the repeated news feed declaring they were in danger. On screen was a new picture, one showing the area directly in front of the hidden hotel. The darkened street crawled with Augers. Milo caught a glimpse of Paul's father among those searching for their sanctuary.

Mrs. Worcestershire's hound-dog face popped into the screen, her beady eyes squinting as she peered in through the window. Milo jolted backward, forgetting the window was one directional. Even though she couldn't see them, it felt as though she was glaring deep into the pit of his soul.

"I think I found it." Her raspy voice floated through the room. The other Augers circled in like scavengers searching for a scrap of meat.

"We're too late," Lily said.

Milo felt like he was in one of those zombie movies, waiting helplessly inside a barricaded fort as the undead came in hordes to break it down, board by board.

"I have an idea." John grabbed the remote powering down the window.

Anything was better than just hanging around waiting for the inevitable. Whatever John had cooked up, Milo was anxious to stop playing defense. No amount of running away from his problems was going to stop Igneous from seeking him out.

Get down there, save them, trust in the power I've granted you. The voice cut through to him and gave him a sense of purpose. He could save them. He was the only one with the power to do so.

John and Lily held back as the others made their way to the elevator. Milo was nervous about splitting up, but it was the only way the plan would work.

Igneous was pretty much invincible as long as he had the Diadem, and he wanted nothing more than to complete it.

The plan made sense, but still, something didn't sit right with Milo. He looked out through the closing metal doors, and John gave him a nod. He could do this. They could do this. Still, he would have been a lot more at ease if he didn't know it meant he had to die.

It became evident something was wrong when the doors to the lobby didn't open immediately.

"Gem Haven is under attack. We are on Level One lockdown. Elevators have been temporarily disabled. In case of fire, please use the stairs. We apologize for any inconvenience," the emotionless mechanical voice repeated.

Mark pried on the metal doors, but couldn't get them to budge. A red light flashed in the cramped room.

"How did they find us? We managed to keep our location a secret for so long." Jade huffed, glaring at a mechanical panel she'd pulled out from a wall.

Milo felt defeated. Not only had his stone played a major role in giving Igneous a target location, if he was working with the Augers, then their incident on the plane was likely a second source of blame.

"All joking aside, I'd like to apologize for earlier. I knew there was nothing between you and Jade." Mark held out a fur-covered paw.

"It's okay." He took the offering and shook hands. He was awed by Mark's sudden serious tone.

"I mean, come on, it's fairly obvious you're obsessed with John. If we get through this, you might want to let him know how you feel." Mark winked.

Milo's face flushed. There's no way he could have been that obvious.

"There it is. Has my little buddy finally stopped denying who he is?" Mark gave him a hard pat on the back, knocking the wind out of him.

"I think I...got it." Jade reconnected a wire and pressed a key on the panel. The flashing lights ceased and the voice faded out.

Milo readied himself, suddenly unable to get John out of his head. He brushed his palm up against the key card in his pocket. Mark backed away, crouching down on all fours as the elevator doors opened to reveal the lobby.

The tiger leapt into the ongoing fray.

The once pristine lobby now lay in shambles as Augers clashed with Lavalieres. One of the crystalline chandeliers lay shattered on the floor, over-turned chairs were being used as barricades, and not a single surface was left without some sign of the ongoing struggle.

Introducing a tiger into the mix provided enough of a distraction for them to dash over to the counter, crouching behind it for cover.

"I didn't see Igneous," Jade said.

"He's here. I can feel it," Milo said. The bloodstone was reacting like mad to his presence.

A cry rang out from one of the Augers. Milo listened to the shouts, hoping to hear a familiar voice he could latch onto for direction. Only two distinct voices registered, those of Riley and Sophia, each coming from opposite ends of the lobby, calling out commands to those defending against the Augers. With their leadership, it looked as though they were managing to stand their ground.

A shadow crept up across the wall, and Milo caught sight of it out of the corner of his vision. No caster could be seen. The arms of the shadow waved frantically, and Milo tried to make out what she was trying to tell them.

A bright white light appeared on the wall, and the shadow stopped. The arms reached in toward her chest to touch it, and her head bowed as though she were looking down at it. The shadow began to dissipate, dissolving from inside out as the area the light touched grew larger.

Milo watched in horror as the shadow disappeared, sensing a devastating finality to the attack.

"No!" Jade jumped up from their hiding spot, shooting dagger after dagger of ice.

Milo knew it was now or never. He hopped over the counter ran out across the floor, hoping to interrupt as many Auger attacks as he could. He raised the bloodstone to generate a lava shield in front of him, but a familiar voice said *Stop.*

Milo turned to face the hooded figure…Igneous.

Milo raised his stone the same way Jade had, hoping he might be able to call forth a fireball or something. Instead, the stone went dark and dormant.

"Not now," he grunted through clenched teeth. He could feel his power, his control over the gem, dissipating as he stood there helpless.

"My dear Milo. I gave you an opportunity to join me. You should have taken me up on that offer while you had the chance." Igneous' corrupt voice rumbled through the lobby, halting the Augers with his grand entrance.

"Never." He tried everything he could think of to activate the bloodstone, but to no avail.

"You didn't really think you had control over your powers," he held up his own bloodstone, "did you?"

Did you? The voice echoed within his head. Milo's eyes widened in realization. This entire time he'd thought he had been getting closer to mastering his bloodstone, but it was all a lie.

"I control your powers."

He laughed and Milo felt his stone activating. A spark shot from his hand, searing a small hole into his shirt.

Milo felt his whole world had come crashing down on him in that moment. Igneous had control over him. He was a tool, a pawn for Igneous to move around to get what he wanted. But why?

Jade skid to a stop a few feet away from Milo, leaving a trail of ice in her path. Her face, covered with little pieces of frozen crystals, sparkled in the light.

Igneous wanted her. And Milo had been dumb enough to lead him straight to her.

"You want my gem? You'll have to forcibly take it from me," she yelled and directed a blizzard in his direction.

Milo's arm rose against his will, and the red shield formed from the bloodstone. The solid magma wall blocked Igneous from the attack.

"Don't you know when to give up? The game is over. You're no match for my powers."

"Those aren't your powers. You stole them. You're the biggest leech there is," she accused.

Milo struggled against the power controlling him, using his free hand to pull the bloodstone down. It was useless. This maniac really was in complete control of him.

He turned to Jade. She knew what she had to do.

Chapter Twelve

"Come on, wake up, we don't have much time before he realizes what happened," Jade said as she shook Milo.

He blinked and looked up at the artificial clouds of the secondary courtyard. A searing pain shot up through his arm from the bloodstone.

"I'm sorry for the theatrics, but I wanted it to at least appear believable." She helped pull him to his feet.

The last thing he remembered was falling into a peaceful sleep in the lobby. Somewhere in the back of his mind, he knew he had to move quickly, but his body wanted to roll over and crawl under a nice warm blanket. He groaned.

"I remember my first regen, slept for about half a day after it. Too bad you don't have that luxury."

"Yeah, too bad. I've already figured that out," he managed between breaths to muster a response with his hands on his hips. He had to recoup quick otherwise their plan wouldn't work. Milo checked his pocket and found the second key card, grateful it had regenerated with him, and even more grateful his clothing had as well.

"Come on, there's another elevator around back," Jade said.

Tricky, tricky. You think you're the first to run from

me? Eeny Meeny Miny Moe, catch a tiger by the toe, if he hollers...good.

"He's got Mark." Milo stumbled unsteadily out into the hallway and heard the raucous noises coming from the lobby. He knew Jade could see his wheels turning. Igneous was in his head, and he couldn't get him out. He pounded his palm against his forehead.

"Stick to the plan," Jade warned, but Milo hesitated.

The plan. They were to head back, and it had made perfect sense at the time. But now, with Mark held captive, he felt as though they had made a mistake.

"I can't..." The choices tugged at him, "I can't leave him."

He handed her the key. He was done running from his problems and putting his friends in constant danger. This was his battle, not Mark's.

"You don't know what he's capable of," she warned.

"I know, but I have to try."

Milo reached the doorway back to the lobby and heard an argument going on inside. Peeking in, he saw Paul's father, face dark red with anger as he approached Igneous.

"We followed you because you said you could destroy these magicks and bring our lives back to normal. You were one of them all along!" he screamed.

"Quiet peon. Your goals were helpful in getting me here, but you've already served your purpose. Leave."

"No! I want my son back. You promised I would have him back."

"I think you misunderstand me. Your requests no longer matter."

Igneous removed his hood and revealed the Diadem, one of the stones on it glowing with radiant light. Paul's father backed away from the grotesque and sickly gray man, but it was too late. A vine of light extended forward, wrapping around the stout man's neck, and squeezed until all signs of life drained from his body.

"Does anyone else dare question me?"

The rest of the Augers backed away, and a few escaped through the front door.

Milo couldn't wait around and let anyone else risk their lives. "You want me? Fine. But leave my friends alone," he announced, shoving himself through the double doors.

"No! It's a trap!" shouted Mark.

Igneous stood in the dead center of the room on top of a pile of broken lobby furniture. Mark cowered at his feet, surrounded by an intense constricting light.

At the wave of Igneous' hand, the light cage shrunk and confined Mark, forcing him down on all fours. The tiger bellowed.

Milo's anger bubbled, and his breathing quickened. If there was ever a time for him to be in control of his powers, now would be nice.

"I said let him go!" Milo called upon his bloodstone, pushing all of his energy into a single thrust. He could picture the red-hot pillar of flame that should have burst from the stone. He could feel the pressure building inside him, but it remained corked.

"Stubborn little nitwit. Never even taught how to do a proper *flourish* technique. Such foolishness," Igneous mocked.

"Some might call it bravery," Milo quipped, giving

a nod to Mark. The tiger delivered a mighty roar and struggled against the constraints. One by one, the links snapped and he leapt away from the mangled cage. Each broken strand of light collapsed and fizzled into the floor.

"I created you. I kept your powers in check. And now you would attempt to turn them against me?"

Milo's skin boiled just beneath the surface. His entire body pulsed, glowing from the internalized buildup of energy. He fell to his knees, wheezing between dry heaves. His body was an incinerator, burning up everything within.

He howled in pain and struggled to regain control, but his willpower began to falter. His heartbeat pounded against his temples, ticking away the remaining seconds before his body could no longer contain the energy.

Small bursts of flames ignited across his body, flaring up, and then burning off. He fell to his back and exploded into a ball of pure heat energy. His skin crackled, popped, and seared.

Through the fire, smoke, and pain, he saw Igneous looming over him. The expression he wore resembled a cat cornering a mouse. The shining crown he wore reflected the flickering flames.

"Can you feel it? Your power will consume your mind until there is nothing left but raw energy. I can stop it. All you have to do is say the word," Igneous offered.

"Please...kill...me..." he choked out. Only the finality of death could release him from such tortuous pain.

"No, you can't fool me twice. This pain will

endure. However, I might be willing to help you control it again, if you tell me where I can find the girl. Join me, Milo. There's no use fighting it."

"Okay, fine!" Milo snapped. He'd do anything to end the pain.

And then it did. Igneous implanted himself firmly as a barrier and controlled Milo's abilities once more. The built up energy dissipated in a series of short bursts of flames dancing across his body.

"Now, where is the girl?" Igneous reached down and helped Milo to his feet, showing no sign of being affected by the fire.

He pointed to the spare key he'd dropped earlier and explained she'd taken refuge in the room.

"You see, you can never really trust anybody. They'll leave you the moment your back is turned. You, on the other hand, are incredibly and almost foolishly loyal. I could use an apprentice such as yourself."

"What makes you think I'd join you?" Milo pulled away from Igneous, considering a new plan of escape.

Mark watched, and Milo found himself in a very difficult situation. Mark stood for everything he believed in, bravery and commitment to friendship. Mark had been willing to sacrifice himself, and fought against Igneous even with the belief it was a losing battle. And now, he was watching to see if Milo could make the same brave choices.

"Because if you don't, I'll release you to a fate worse than death."

While keeping his eyes locked on Mark, he confirmed his choice to join Igneous. Mark's features sagged, his shoulders hunched. He shook his head and mouthed "no."

"Good boy."

A chain of light shot out to Mark, wrapping around the tiger's neck. A surge rushed through Milo as he felt the urge to help his friend. But if he tried, Igneous would surely release the bloodstone in the process. Mark struggled against the chain as he was pulled down to the floor.

"Are you going to kill him?" Milo asked.

"Not yet. I want him to witness you turning on each of your friends first. Until then, he's nothing more than a pet." Igneous roped in the leash, pulling the tiger to his side. "But if he attempts to struggle or even act human, I'll gladly turn this chain into a choker." He emphasized his point by tightening the length around Mark's neck.

Mark bellowed in defeat. With the tiger in tow, Igneous followed as Milo led the way toward his ultimate betrayal.

****

Milo sighed as they approached his hotel room. He wished he could warn his friends about what they were going to be up against. Mark gave him a pleading look, but Milo ignored his friend, took a deep breath, and unlocked the door.

A latch caught, preventing the door from opening much more than a couple of inches. He silently celebrated this tiny victory. It wouldn't last long, but hopefully this would slow Igneous down long enough for them to prepare.

"Pitiful," Igneous said, and Milo felt his arm rising, the bloodstone pulsed, and released a burst of flame that melted through the chain.

So much for that roadblock.

Mark leapt into the room, dragging Igneous along by the chain. Milo jumped in and closed the door behind them, yelling "now!"

John jumped out of his hiding spot, brandishing the remote control like a weapon. With the flip of a switch, the screened window came to life, displaying the vast and empty desert surface of the moon.

Igneous was pulled into the air like a kite on a string. The sudden shift in gravity caught him off guard. Mark bounded off a wall and shifted direction, pulling Igneous along with him. The Diadem flung off its perch, clattering against the wall, and with it, the light chain connecting Mark to Igneous disappeared.

Milo's arm rose and pointed at John. A pillar of fire shot out and enveloped the unprepared kid. Milo screamed as he watched the charred body drop slowly to the floor, the remote melting as it fell with him.

A small electrical buzz discharged from the remote and the screen shut off. Gravity returned to normal, dropping Igneous to his knees.

"Foolish kids. You'll pay for that." He reached up to activate a stone from the Diadem only just realizing it wasn't there.

"Looking for this?" Jade asked, holding up the prized jeweled crown.

Igneous scowled, and Milo felt himself shift in her direction. At this rate, he was going to be used to pick off his friends, one at a time. He struggled against the control, feeling even more hopeless in the fight against it than the first time.

Mark pounced, knocked into Milo and sent the fire into the window. It cracked the screen and left behind a large scorch mark.

Jade stood resolute as a statue, directing her own power against Igneous.

Without the Diadem, Igneous appeared significantly weakened and unable to defend against the blast of icy water that began to encase him.

Milo heard Igneous screaming inside his head and felt a last ditch attempt to have Milo melt the layers of ice.

Lily stepped out from the shadows and placed her hand on his. The room compressed, reacting to her hematite.

His body reacted to the intrusion, recognizing her attack, and attempted to defend itself from her. A bubble of fire surrounded him, restricting Igneous' control.

A rush of energy forced Milo to retreat within his own mind, allowing the bloodstone to react purely on instinct. The fires resumed, consuming him in the process, eating away at the recesses of his memory.

Igneous had left him to die.

Chapter Thirteen

Milo awoke with a start. A searing pain shot through his hand up to his elbow. He took away a small amount of joy from his discomfort. At least he wasn't dead, or insane.

"Take it easy." Pavlovian stood at the foot of his bed. The cracked window screen and the lingering smell of charred wood filled the room. Had he even left? It didn't matter.

"Don't worry about the damages. I'll have this room fixed up in a jiffy," Pavlovian said and with the wave of his gem, the damages reverted, restoring the room back to the way it looked when Milo first arrived.

If he hadn't known any better, he never would have believed a major battle with Igneous occurred there.

"Did we win?" he asked, managing a smile. John's plan made sense, but even then it was hard to believe they could actually pull it off.

Lily held his hand clasped between hers, a glowing white aura surrounding them both. His fingers tingled, a sensation he'd usually associate with his arm falling asleep.

He jumped and pulled his arm away, not wanting his gem power to activate in response and hurt those around him. The numbness went away, and the pain increased tenfold, raw skin outlined a hole in his hand where glistening pink skin bubbled with blood. The bloodstone was gone.

"Calm." Nina's voice floated on the air like a hot air balloon and his body eased.

"What? Where's my…?"

He managed to start, feeling like he was in a dentist's chair being administered anesthetic. Lily took his hands again and continued working toward closing the wound.

"We did it. We got Igneous," Jade explained, coming up to the foot of his bed. "It's all thanks to you. You pulled off the best ruse ever."

"We had to remove the bloodstone," Pavlovian explained. "I suspected Igneous had some kind of control over your powers. Once he relinquished that control, you had no means of controlling the bond."

Milo felt the weight of his loss. No bloodstone meant no powers, which in turn meant he was no longer a Lavaliere. Surrounded by his friends, each with their own special abilities, he couldn't help but feel like he'd lost the one thing that helped him belong and kept him an outcast. Without it, he was left solely with the title of outcast.

"I'm so sorry. I tried to fight him," Milo uttered as many apologies as he could manage.

"The Diadem is safe." Mark swaggered into the room and handed a special looking key card over to Pavlovian.

"Thanks…and will you please consider putting on some pants?" Pavlovian's voice was full of disgust.

"No way, José." Mark pounced on the couch.

Pavlovian averted his gaze, glaring at Jade. "Why did you ever tell him my first name?"

He scoffed and turned to Milo. "In order to get the

bloodstone out of you, we had to fuse it with the Diadem, which was part of Igneous' plan all along. Unfortunately, this means the Diadem is one step closer to completion and that much more dangerous."

"What about my powers?" Milo asked, hoping there would be some way to get them back.

"Gone, they were artificial to begin with," Pavlovian answered.

Milo had already prepared himself for that inevitability, but the confirmation made it final. "And Igneous?"

"Riley took care of him." Pavlovian replied.

Confused, Milo began to inquire about how Riley became involved, but his question was brushed aside.

"You need not concern yourself. Everything will be taken care of. Get some rest and let Lily take care of that hand of yours."

Milo lay back on the bed and gave his hand back to Lily. He strained to distinguish her familiar *flourish,* but there was nothing, no immediate sense of the universe listening in. He watched as his skin pulled taught, hardening to help mend his wound, then a tingling sensation spread through his palm, gradually diminishing his pain. After, a dark bloody scab was all that remained to serve as a distant memory of the bloodstone and the life that had been forced on him.

He ran a finger over the sensitive new flesh. For a short time, the stone had made him special—one of a kind. And throughout most of that time, he'd wanted nothing more than to get rid of it, to cast it away and try again. Now he felt empty and naked, stripped of the power he'd come to rely on.

"Where is the Diadem now?" Milo asked

Pavlovian as casually as he could manage.

"It's locked up somewhere safe, and I'm the only one with a key. You don't have to worry about it anymore."

"Why not just destroy it?" he asked.

"With all of the stones fused into it as protection, an attempt would surely be thwarted by at least one of the passive abilities," Pavlovian explained.

This interested Milo, who contemplated the implications of Pavlovian's statement. Did that mean bonded gems didn't need a host? One thing Milo knew for certain, he needed to get his bloodstone back.

"Get some rest," Pavlovian said as Lily wrapped a bandage around his hand. "You performed admirably."

And yet it wasn't good enough. Memories of Igneous forcing him to use his powers came flooding back like a broken dam. He'd taken his friend's life with his own hands. He'd killed John. And he'd never had the chance to tell him how he truly felt.

"I'm fine by the way, thanks for asking," Mark scoffed.

The poorly timed comment compounded Milo's pain, and hit him like a punch in the ribs. He understood they won, but it didn't feel that way. Didn't comic book stories always end on a high note?

"Did I forget to mention that he's okay, too?" Mark winked and pointed over to the door.

Milo followed his gaze, blinking to hold back his tears. John! He jumped off the bed and tackled the boy he thought he'd lost forever.

"I'm so sorry, I never meant for any of that to happen." Milo felt his friend tense up in his arms and he stepped back. John hadn't said a word yet, and Milo worried his friend had been trying to keep himself hidden behind Mark.

John lowered his head, his silence was deafening. Pavlovian's words rang out, both reminding and taunting him. *"Physical pain is only temporary, emotional scars last a lifetime."* He'd given up and allowed Igneous to take control over his body, control he'd used to hurt John.

"Can you forgive me?" He hoped it wasn't too late to correct himself. John gave a small nod, still not bringing himself to say anything. It was better than nothing. The small gesture meant there was at least room for him to make up for what he'd done.

"I love you," he whispered, allowing his chin to rest in the crook of John's neck. He closed his eyes and hoped this moment would last him a lifetime.

"I love you, too." John pulled him into the embrace, and a magic far more powerful than any gem bond washed away Milo's pain.

A word about the author...

Nicholas began reading at the age of three, and not long after that, began writing as well. Years later, he found an interest in young adult fantasy and, early on, finished the draft of his first full-length novel in 2006.

Nicholas strives to write at least one full-length novel each year and hopes to someday be a household name...at the very least, inside the homes of his friends and family.